JN437272

유형의 땅

아시아에서는 《바이링궐 에디션 한국 대표 소설》을 기획하여 한국의 우수한 문학을 주제별로 엄선해 국내외 독자들에게 소개합니다. 이 기획은 국내외 우수한 번역가들이 참여하여 원작의 품격을 최대한 살렸습니다. 문학을 통해 아시아의 정체성과 가치를 살피는 데 주력해 온 아시아는 한국인의 삶을 넓고 깊게 이해하는 데 이 기획이 기여하기를 기대합니다.

Asia Publishers presents some of the very best modern Korean literature to readers worldwide through its new Korean literature series 〈Bi-lingual Edition Modern Korean Literature〉. We are proud and happy to offer it in the most authoritative translation by renowned translators of Korean literature. We hope that this series helps to build solid bridges between citizens of the world and Koreans through a rich in-depth understanding of Korea.

바이링궐 에디션 한국 대표 소설 005

Bi-lingual Edition Modern Korean Literature 005

The Land of the Banished

조정래
유형의 땅

Jo Jung-rae

ASIA PUBLISHERS

Contents

유형의 땅

The Land of the Banished

"이 늙고 천헌 목심 편히게 눈감을 수 있도록 선상님, 지발 굽어살펴 주씨요. 요러크름 빌 팅께요."

영감은 부처님 앞에 합장을 할 때보다 더 간절하고 애타는 심정으로 손을 모았고, 그것도 부족한 것 같아 그만 바닥에 무릎까지 꿇었다.

"영감님, 왜 이러십니까. 딱한 사정 충분히 알았으니 어서 의자로 올라앉으십시오."

원장은 당황한 몸짓으로 영감을 일으켜 세우려 했다.

"선상님, 지발 딱 부러지게 맡아 주시겄다고 말씸해 주시씨요."

영감은 몸을 더욱 오그리며 애원하고 있었다.

"Please, sir, let me close my eyes and leave this miserable life in peace. I pray, please help me. I'm begging you."

The old man rubbed his palms together as ardently as if he had been prostrate before a statue of the Buddha. He sank to his knees on the floor in still more abject supplication.

"My good man, there is no call for this. I fully understand your lamentable predicament. Please, get up and have a seat."

With some embarrassment, the Director gestured for the old man to rise.

"Sir, please give me your word that you'll agree to

"……알겠어요. 맡도록 하지요."

원장은 착잡한 표정으로 어렵게 대답했다.

"고맙구만이라, 선상님. 이 하늘 같은 은혜 저시상에 가서라도 잊어 뿔지 않컸구만이라."

가슴께에 두 손을 모으고 무릎을 꿇고 앉은 자세로 영감은 두 번 세 번 고개를 주억거렸다. 그런 영감의 눈에는 안개빛의 눈물이 번지고 있었다.

"영감님, 어서 의자로 올라앉으세요."

이렇게 사정을 하지 않고 문 앞에 버리고 가 버렸으면 어차피 맡아야 될 아이가 아닌가 하고 원장은 생각했다.

어려운 몸짓으로 의자에 다시 앉은 영감은 연상 콧물을 들이마시며 속주머니를 더듬어댔다.

"선상님, 요거 지가 가진 전 재산인디 받아 주시씨요. 뼁아리 오줌 같은 것인디…… 지 맴 표시니께……."

영감의 투박한 손에는 접었던 자리가 선명한 만 원권 지폐 두 장이 들려 있었다.

"아닙니다. 영감님 약값에나 보태십시오. 애는 우리가 다 알아서 할 겁니다."

"지발 받아 주시씨요. 못난 애비의 마지막 맴이니께요. 요걸 안 받으시면 지가 워찌 발길을 돌릴 수 있겄는가요.

take this charge."

The old man seemed to shrink as he renewed his entreaties.

"Very well. I'll see to it."

A look of resignation on his face, the Director responded with reluctance.

"Thank you ever so much, sir. Even in the next world I will remain eternally grateful for your boundless benevolence."

The old man, still on his knees, bowed repeatedly with his hands clasped over his heart. A mist of tears made his eyes shine.

"Enough, please, come back now to your chair."

The Director thought that the old man could have simply left the child at the gate. He would still have been taken in the boy.

After awkwardly taking his seat once more, the old man began fumbling for something in his pocket, sniffling loudly.

"Sir, this is all I have, please accept it. It's no more than chicken feed... only a token from my heart..." Two ten thousand won notes lay creased in the old man's palm.

"Certainly not! Spend it on your medicine. We will provide everything for the child."

선상님. 받아 주시씨요."

눈물이 그렁거리는 영감의 눈은 입보다 몇 곱절 더 애타게 말하고 있었다.

"정 그러시다면……."

원장은 떨리는 영감의 손에서 돈을 옮겨 받았다.

"요건 내복 한 벌썩 장만헌 것이구만이라."

영감은 손등으로 눈을 쓱 문지르고는 조그만 보퉁이 하나를 내밀었다.

"예에……."

원장은 보퉁이를 받아들며 부정(父情)의 신음을 듣고 있었다.

"겉옷도 한 벌썩 장만혔어야 허는디, 속옷을 새로 사 입히고 봉께로 돈이 모지래서……."

영감은 입 언저리에 울음을 가득 물고는 변명처럼 말했다.

"너무 걱정 안 하셔도 됩니다."

"그라고 요것 잘 간수혀 주시씨요."

영감은 낡아 빠진 종이쪽을 조심스럽게 내밀었다. 원장은 종이쪽지에 그리다시피 쓴 '아부지 천만석'이란 여섯 글자를 한눈에 읽었다.

"고것이 지 이름 석 자구만이라. 지 할아부지가 상것으

"Please, sir, accept it as the last request of a wayward father. How can I turn and walk away if you refuse it? Take it. Please."

The man's moist eyes were far more eloquent than his words.

"If you insist..."

The Director accepted the money from the old man's quaking hands.

"And here is a set of underwear for the boy."

Mopping his eyes with the back of his hand, the old man pushed forward a small bundle.

"I see..."

Taking the bundle, the Director heard a painful moan of paternal love.

"I ought to have bought him a full outfit, but after buying these, there just wasn't enough money left over..."

The feeble excuse was accompanied by another break in the old man's voice; he was on the verge of full-blown tears.

"You really needn't worry so."

"And please, keep this as well."

The old man carefully presented a worn piece of paper to the Director.

The Director glanced at the almost illegible charac-

로 가난허게 산 것이 원이 되고 한이 되야, 니만은 꼭 만석꾼 부자가 돼야 쓴다 허고 붙여 준 이름인 모양인디 요꼬라지가 되야 뿌렀소."

영감은 절망의 덩어리 같은 한숨을 내쉬었다.

"새끼 하나 수발 못허는 빙신 같은 애비지만 이름 석 자만은 알게 혀야 되잖을까 혀서……."

"그러믄요. 아버지 없는 자식이 어디서 생겨날 수 있겠습니까. 당연히 알아야 될 일이지요."

원장은 이렇게 말하며 다시 영감을 뜯어보았다. 삶에 지칠 대로 지친, 가랑잎처럼 그 목숨이 사그라들고 있는 한 사내의 운명이 비참하게 놓여 있었다.

영감은 복도에 나가 있는 아들을 불러들였다. 여섯 살이라고는 했지만 제대로 먹이지를 못해서 그런지 가뭄철의 개똥참외처럼 말라비틀어져 있었다. 그런 아이놈의 몰골을 보자 새로운 서러움이 영감의 가슴을 찢었다.

죽으나 사나 끝까지 옆에 끼고 있을걸 잘못한 짓이 아닐까 하는 생각이 불현듯 들었다. 이곳을 찾아오기 전까지 무수히 되풀이했던 아비로서의 죄책감이었다.

"아무리 살기가 어려웠다 해도 몸이 이렇게 되도록 내버려 두면 어떡합니까. 앞으로 아주 조심하셔야 해요. 자

ters scribbled on the sheet: 'Father: Ch'ŏn Man-sŏk.'

"My name, that's what it is. My grandfather came from dirt poor serf stock, so they gave me the name 'Man-sŏk' (a ten thousand bushel harvest) in the hopes I'd make a fortune, but..." A despairing sigh issued from the old man.

"Though I failed the boy, I figured he should at least know his father's name..."

"Of course. There can be no son without a father. Naturally, he should be told."

As he spoke, the Director scrutinized the old man once more. The unhappy fate of this man, used up and withering like a fallen leaf, unfolded itself before his eyes.

The old man called his son in from the corridor.

Although the boy was already six years of age, he was puny, like a drought-shriveled melon. At the sight of him, the old man was plunged once more into sorrow.

Suddenly, it struck the old man that bringing his son to this place might have been a mistake, that he should have stuck with the boy, regardless of what was to come. This thought, stimulated by fatherly guilt, was one he had mulled over a thousand times before finally deciding to bring the boy here.

칫 잘못하다 큰일 납니다."

의사의 이 말이 아들을 끝까지 데리고 있어야 되겠다는 물기 젖은 생각을 동강내고는 했다. 뼈만 얼기설기 드러나는 그 엑스레이라는 흉측한 사진은 자신의 목숨이 기름 바닥난 등잔불 같다고 의사에게 가르쳐 준 모양이었다.

굳이 병원을 찾아가기 전에도 영감은 자신의 병이 얼마나 깊어지고 있나를 대체로 알고 있었다. 입에서 피가 넘어오기 전에 벌써 그 징조는 나타났던 것이다. 이상하다 싶게 몸이 술에 휘둘렸고, 하루가 다르게 기운 쓰기가 어려워졌던 것이다. 기운을 써서 세 끼 밥을 먹고 살아가는 축들은 건강의 변화를 의사보다 더 빨리 눈치채는 재주들을 가지고 있었다.

어느 노동판, 어느 길목에서 숨결이 끊길지 모를 일이었다. 그때 가서 고아로 버려지기는 마찬가지였다. 앞으로 일 년을 더 살게 될지, 이 년을 더 살게 될지 알 수가 없는 일이다. 자신의 손으로 미리 고아원에 맡기는 것이 그나마 한 가닥 핏줄을 지킬 수 있는 유일한 방법이라고 생각했던 것이다.

"철수야, 오늘부텀은 이 원장 선상님허고 여그서 사는 것잉께, 원장 선상님 말씀 잘 들어야 써, 알겠어?"

"No matter how badly life has treated you, you shouldn't have neglected yourself to this extent. From now on, you really must take better care of yourself. There will be no second chances if you don't."

These words from the physician had cut through his desire to stay with the child. From the X-rays he'd taken, the doctor judged that the old man's life was like a flickering lamp with but a few drops of kerosene left to burn.

Even before visiting the clinic, the old man had known his condition was grave. The symptoms had grown progressively worse, until finally he'd begun coughing up blood. The tiniest sip of alcohol proved to be too much, and with each passing day he grew weaker and weaker, making work an ever greater ordeal. Those who earn their daily bread by manual labor usually notice such changes immediately, without needing to be told by any doctor.

You can never tell in advance which street corner or job site will be your last. Sooner or later, the boy would end up alone, an orphan. There was no telling how much longer the old man would live: perhaps a year, perhaps two. Taking the boy to the orphanage himself was the only way he could be

영감은 아들의 조그만 얼굴을 허리 굽혀 깊이 들여다보며 말했다.

"아부지는……?"

아이는 늙은 아버지의 눈을 쳐다보며 짧게 물었다.

"어허, 또 그 소리. 느그 엄니 찾아갖고 온다고 쌔 빠지게 헌 말 잊어뿌렀냐?"

영감은 일부러 사나운 목소리로 말했다.

"언제 와?"

아이는 시무룩해져서, 그러나 아버지의 눈을 똑바로 쳐다본 채로 물었다.

"엄니 찾으면 금시 올 것잉께……."

"못 찾으면?"

아이는 아버지의 말을 자르며 다부지게 물었다.

영감은 잠시 말문이 막혔다. 가슴 저 깊이로 서러움 한 줄기가 싸늘하게 뻗쳐 나갔다.

"올 것이여, 엄니 찾아갖고 꼭 와."

영감은 자신 있게 말했다.

"아부지, 약속 걸어."

아이는 새끼손가락을 내밀었다. 영감은 손가락을 내밀 생각도 않고 아들을 물끄러미 바라보고 있었다.

certain that his bloodline would go on.

"Dear Ch'ŏl-su, from this day on you'll be living here with this good gentleman. Better listen well and do what he says, understand?"

As he spoke, the old man stooped and peered into his son's tiny face.

"And what will you do, Father?" asked the boy at once, looking directly into his father's eyes.

"Ah, ah, not that again. Already forgotten that I'll be coming back once I've found your mom?"

The old man's voice rasped with feigned severity.

"When'll you come back'?" the boy asked again, downcast but still gazing straight into the old man's eyes.

"Just as soon as I find her..."

"But what if you can't?" interrupted the child.

For a second the old man was at a loss for words. He felt a dagger of ice-cold grief piercing his soul.

"I'll be coming with your mother, without fail," he finally replied, his voice full of confidence.

"Promise, Dad?"

The boy extended his little finger to seal the pact. Oblivious to the child's gesture, the old man just stared blankly at his son's face.

Poor little thing. Such an ill-starred fate to come

불쌍한 내 새끼. 어쩌다 나 같은 인종한테 태어나 요런 꼴이 된단 말이냐. 건강허게 커야 써. 아프지 말고. 밥 잘 묵고…… 불쌍한 내 새끼…….

"빨리 약속 걸어."

"그려, 그려."

영감은 주체할 수 없이 솟구치는 울음의 덩이를 목이 찢어지도록 아프게 삼키며 손가락을 내밀었다.

작고 가느다란 손가락과 굵고 투박한 손가락이 허공에서 얽혀졌다.

"아부지, 엄니 찾아서 꼭 와야 해."

아이가 손가락에 힘을 주고 손을 흔들며 말했다.

"그려, 그려."

"엄니 빨랑 찾아 달라고 밤마다 기도할 거야."

"그려, 그려."

영감은 이제 울음을 질겅질겅 씹고 있었다.

똑똑헌 내 새끼야. 니 혼자 앞으로 어쩌크름 살 것이냐. 요런 생이별을 알았으면 낳지를 말았어야 혔는디. 이 못난 애비가…… 불쌍헌 내 새끼야…….

"철수야, 원장 선생님 말씸 잘 들어야 혀. 여그서는 밥 굶는 일도 읎고, 가마니 깔고 자는 일도 읎어. 아부지허고

into the world with a father like me. Have to grow up strong, now. Stay healthy, eat well... my poor little one...

"Hurry, Dad, give me your finger to fix the promise."

"Okay, okay."

The old man offered his finger, swallowing the lump that was rising in his throat. The thin little pinky of the boy and the thick, gnarled finger of the old man clasped one another.

"Dad, you've got to find Mom and come back to me!" the child cried, wrapping his finger tighter around his father's.

"Sure, sure."

"I'll pray every night so you can find Mom soon."

"Right, right."

By this time the old man was grinding the tears back with his jaw.

My smart little one. How will you ever make it alone? If I'd known it would come to this, I never would have let you be born. Fool of a father... my poor little one...

"Dear Ch'ŏl-su, remember, you must listen to the Director, he's a fine man. Here, you'll never go hungry. You'll never have to sleep on a straw mat. It'll

살 때보담 훨씬 좋으니께 원장 선상님 말씸 잘 들어야 혀. 알겄어?"

아이는 이별이 가까워진 것을 느끼는지 시무룩한 표정으로 고개만 끄덕였다.

"자아, 철수야, 이리 오너라."

원장이 이별을 알렸다.

영감은 아이와 얽었던 손가락을 풀고 일어섰다. 그리고 아이의 등을 밀어 원장에게로 보냈다. 아이의 여윈 등은 밀리지 않으려고 저항하고 있었고, 그 기운은 영감의 손바닥을 타고 들어 뜨겁게 전신으로 퍼져 나가고 있었다.

"너무 걱정 마십시오."

원장 이별을 재촉하고 있었다.

"그저 잘, 잘……."

영감은 두 번 세 번 머리를 조아렸고, 끝내 말끝을 맺지 못했다.

영감은 다 헐어빠진 가방을 드는가 싶더니 급하게 돌아서서 사무실을 나섰다.

"아부지!"

영감은 뒤돌아보지 않았다.

복도를 지나 운동장으로 나섰다. 영감은 휘적휘적 걸으

be far better than living with your daddy, so you must always do what the Director tells you, do you hear me?"

Sensing that the parting was near, the child nodded, lowering his eyes.

"Now, Ch'ŏl-su, come on over here," the Director said, marking the moment of farewell.

The old man unclasped his finger and stood. He nudged the boy's back, pushing him over toward the Director. In his palm he could feel the resistance coming from the scrawny back of the child, and the small pressure flooded through his entire being.

"Please, don't worry yourself too much," the Director said, seeking to speed the inevitable separation.

"Please, I beg you..."

The old man bowed several times but was incapable of finishing the sentence. He picked up his ragged bag and rushed out of the office.

"Dad!"

The old man didn't look back.

He passed through the hall and burst out onto the playground. Staggering along, he finally broke into the long awaited sobs.

"Daaad!!! Bring Mom and come back! You must

며 비로소 눈물을 쏟고 있었다.

"아부지이이, 엄니 찾아서 꼭 와야 해애!"

운동장을 다 지나 정문께에 이르렀을 때 아들놈의 외침이 뒤에서 쟁쟁하게 들려왔다. 영감은 뒤돌아보지 않으려 했지만 도저히 되지 않는 일이었다.

돌아섰다. 아들은 원장에게 어깨를 잡힌 채 현관에 서서 손을 흔들고 있었다.

"꼭 와야 해애, 아부지이이!"

영감은 다시 솟구치는 울음을 울며 돌아섰다.

"오살을 헐 년, 저 불쌍한 새끼를 내뻘고 도망을 치다니……."

영감은 부르르 몸서리를 치며 이빨을 앙다물었다.

여편네의 헤실헤실 웃는 얼굴이 눈물로 흐려진 눈앞에 떠올랐다.

"나쁜 년 같으니라고!"

바로 눈앞에 상대가 있기라도 한 듯 욕을 쏴대며 손등으로 눈을 쓱 문질렀다. 여편네의 모습은 간 곳이 없었다.

영감의 가슴에서는 다시 불길 같은 증오가 타올랐다. 잡기만 하면 정말 두 연놈을 그대로 살려 두지 않을 결심으로 네 살짜리 어린것을 들쳐 업고 방방곡곡을 헤매며

come back!!!"

His son's wails could be heard clearly as he crossed the playground and approached the main gate. The old man tried to keep on going but could not. He turned back around. The boy was at the front door, waving to him as the Director grasped his shoulders.

"Be sure to come back, Dad?"

The old man once more turned to leave, weeping as he went.

"Filthy bitch! To run off and abandon the poor kid!"

The old man shuddered, his teeth clenched. His wife's grinning face appeared before his tear-fogged eyes.

"Rotten bitch!!!"

He swore, as if she were right in front of him, then wiped his eyes with the back of his hand. The image of his wife evaporated into thin air.

A flame of hatred came alive within him once again, the same flame that had burned back in those days. Two long years had passed since he had set out with the four-year-old boy on his back, searching the countryside and vowing that, if he ever caught up with the bitch and her bastard of a

이 년을 보낸 것이다.

"내가 넋 빠진 잡놈이었어."

영감은 절망적인 한숨을 내쉬었다. 여편네에 대한 식을 줄 모르는 증오심과 똑같은 비중으로 후회의 자책감도 함께 마음을 괴롭히는 것이었다.

집도 절도 없는 막노동꾼 신세에 무슨 영화를 보자고 꽃을 볼 작정을 했었는지 몰랐다. 자신의 일이었으면서도 도무지 이해가 되지 않았다. 그만큼 그 일은 후회스러운 것이었고, 그때 일만 저지르지 않았더라면 이제 와서 핏줄을 남의 손에 맡기는 일은 하지 않아도 되었을 것이라는 안타까움이 영감을 못 견디게 하고 있었다.

"천 씨는 이 나이가 되도록 왜 혼자 살아요? 외롭지 않아요?"

여자가 이런 식으로 꼬리를 치기 시작했을 때 모질게 잘랐어야 했다. 그런데 비린내 맡은 고양이처럼 회가 동해 가고 있었다.

"그렇게 말허는 임자는 왜 혼자 산당가? 그라고, 외롭지 않다는 것잉가?"

이렇게 대꾸하며 색다르게 느껴지는 여자 냄새에 코를 벌름거리지 않았던가.

lover, they'd never escape him alive.

"A spineless bastard, that's what I've been," sighed the old man in despair. The unrelenting rage he felt toward his wife was matched only by his self-loathing. He no longer had any idea how he could ever have imagined that marriage might hold any real happiness for a homeless day laborer like himself. Though it had been his own choice, he never fully understood it. And now he was constantly tortured by the thought that this pain of committing his own flesh and blood to the care of strangers might have been avoided back then.

"Why have you been living alone all these years? Don't you get lonely?"

As soon as the woman took to wagging her tail like that, he should have cut it off, showing no softness. But like a cat exposed to the odor of fish, he had been intoxicated instead.

"Well, why do you live on your own, when you talk like that?" he'd replied. "You mean you never get lonesome?" And yet, even as he bantered back, hadn't his nostrils flared at her scent?

"I live this hard life alone because nobody will have me. With a fate as unfortunate as mine, there's

"데려갈 사람이 없으니 이런 모진 고생 해 가며 혼자 사는 거지요. 나 같은 박복한 신세, 외로워도 어쩔 수 있나요."

여자는 갑자기 기가 팍 꺾이며 말했고, 그는 불현듯 여자가 불쌍하다는 생각을 하면서 가슴이 울렁거리는 것을 느꼈다.

이 무신 느자구 읎는 짓거리여. 반평생을 하루같이 쫓기고 숨어 살아온 체신에 무신 놈에 암내는 맡고 지랄이여.

그는 자신의 꿈틀거리고 흔들리려는 마음을 황급하게 다잡고는 했다. 끝까지 그렇게 했어야 했다. 그렇지 못할 것 같았으면 그 공사판을 일찍이 등졌어야 했다.

공사판은 기름기가 자르르 돌고 있었다. 겨울철 같지 않게 일거리는 지천으로 널려 있었다. 공단(工團)은 내년 봄에 가동하도록 되어 있었고, 직원들이 입주할 아파트도 그때까지 짓지 않으면 안 될 형편이었다. 그래서 일거리는 남아도는 판이었고, 일당도 후한 데다가 지불도 시간을 어기는 일조차 없을 지경이었다.

삼십 년이 다 차 가도록 오만가지 공사판을 찾아 떠돌아다녔지만 이처럼 걸직한 판은 만난 적이 없었다. 그것도 겨울철에 말이다. 공사판이 이렇듯 기름진 것이 또 하

nothing to be done about being lonely," she said, her voice suddenly dispirited. He felt his heart throb with pity for the woman.

What a waste it's all been, he thought, half my life spent hiding, and now here I am in a mindless tit, captivated by the mere smell of this female.

More often than not he was able to put a stop to his mind's wavering before it was too late, but that time he had failed. Rather than lose control of himself, he should have just quit that job and left that town.

But the construction projects in those parts were a gold mine to a job-hungry man. There was plenty of work to be had, not like the normal winter season. A new industrial park had been scheduled to open by the following spring, and many blocks of workers' housing needed to be finished by then. There were as much work as you liked and decent wages, and even better, the contractors paid the wages generally on time. Nearly thirty years of drifting from job to job, and never before had he run across one like this, not to mention in the depths of winter. Still, such a well-paid job was not without its hazards.

"Life is a blink of an eye, Mr. Ch'ŏn, and what

나 탈이라면 탈이었다.

"사람 한평생 잠깐인데 천 씨는 무슨 재미로 살아요?"

"거 무신 씨나락 까묵는 소리랑가?"

"이렇게 밤마다 쏘주 마시는 재미?"

여자는 술을 따라 주며 빠끔하게 쳐다보았다.

"재미로 술 마시는 사람도 있능가? 재미가 읎으니께 술이나 푸제."

"그럼 기막힌 재미를 만들면 되잖아요."

"무신 기맥힌 재미는…… 하루 벌어 하루 묵는 신세에."

가당찮다는 듯 그는 술을 입에 털어 넣고는 깍두기를 으석으석 씹었다.

"하루 벌어 하루 먹는 신세라고 누가 색시 재미, 자식 재미 못 보게 막던가요? 사람 사는 게 뭔데 천 씨는 이 나이가 되도록 마누라 하나, 자식 하나 없어요? 천 년 살 줄 알지만 이러다 더 나이 먹고, 덜컥 병이나 나 봐요. 아니, 죽으면 송장은 누가 거둬 주고, 찬물 한 사발이라도 제사는 누가 지내 준답디까. 이 세상에서 공사판 찾아 떠돌이 인생 살았으니 저세상에 가서도 떠돌이 귀신 돼야겠단 말인가요?"

pleasure does it give you?"

"What the devil are you talking about?"

"Do you live for the pleasure of drinking *soju* every night? Like this?"

The woman stared at him as she refilled his glass.

"Does a man drink for pleasure? Doesn't he drink to drown his sorrows?"

"Can't you find any real pleasure, then'?"

"Real pleasure? What... for a common day laborer?"

Trying to ignore the absurdity of the exchange, he gulped down his drink and loudly chewed his radish *kimchi.*

"Who keeps you from having the pleasure of a wife and children, day laborer or nor? What kind of a life is it, after all, single and childless at your age? You may think you'll live for a thousand years, but what if you suddenly wake up to find yourself old and sick? Who'll bury you when you're gone, and who'll remember you as an ancestor? Just because you've been a drifter in this life doesn't mean you have to go on drifting in the next as well."

"What? Such nonsense out of that beak of yours!"

And yet even as he shouted, he felt an uncanny chill.

"멋이여? 무신 놈에 주둥아리를 고러크름 싸가지 읎이 나불대?"

그는 섬뜩함을 느끼며 소리를 버럭 질렀다.

"어머, 무서워라. 화내지 말고 생각해 봐요. 지금 천 씨 나이에 홀몸인데 내 말이 틀렸나를요."

"듣기 싫여. 문딩이 보고 문딩이라고 놀리니께 화가 나는 것이여."

"그럼 지금이라도 늦지 않았으니 문딩이 신세를 면하면 될 거 아네요."

"멋이라고……?"

그는 바로 코앞에서 헤시시 웃고 있는 여자의 발그레한 눈자위를 보면서 불두덩에 찌르르 전기가 통하는 것을 느꼈다.

순임이는 국밥집에서 일을 하고 있었다. 그래서 하루에 한 번씩은 꼭 대하곤 했다. 그저 흩어져 있는 소문으로는 시집을 갔다가 내쫓겼고, 국밥집은 먼 친척이 된다는 정도였다. 한 가지 분명한 것은, 어느 공사판에든 걸레처럼 널려 있는 작부는 아니었다.

만석은 순임이의 말을 듣고 새삼스럽게 자신의 신세를 돌이켜보지 않을 수 없었다. 순임이는 자신의 아픈 데를

"Goodness, you frightened me. Don't be angry, just think it over. Alone at your age! Just ask yourself whether or not what I'm saying is true."

"Cut it out! Call a leper a leper and see if he isn't enraged, why don't you!"

"Well, it's not too late to escape a leper's fate."

"What...?"

And as he gazed at the corners of the woman's laughing eyes he felt a pulse of electricity in his groin.

Sun-im worked in the dive of a canteen that had been thrown up at the jobsite, and so he saw her face every day. He knew nothing about her, nothing except a rumor that she'd been kicked out by her husband and ended up at this canteen because it was run by a distant relative. But one thing was clear: she wasn't the sort of whore one usually found strewn about these worksites like so many used rags.

On hearing Sun-im's words, Man-sŏk couldn't help looking back over his life. As if armed with a pair of pincers, she had probed his most painful wounds. It wasn't that he hadn't been troubled before meeting her, but he had always been able to do his best to forget, to keep the pain out of his mind. And from

족집게처럼 찍어 낸 것이었다. 순임이가 아니더라도 전에 언뜻언뜻 생각하지 않은 건 아니었다. 그러나 애써 잊어버리려고, 생각하지 않으려고 해 왔었다. 그런 생각이 스친 날이면 다른 날과는 달리 곤죽이 되도록 술을 마셨다.

삼십 년으로 기울기 시작한 세월에 이르는 동안 공사판을 찾아 정처 없이 떠돌면서 겪은 여자는 무수하게 많았다. 정이 있어 엮어진 사이가 아니라 돈을 주고받고 얽힌 사이였다. 막노동꾼이 인간쓰레기라면 그 쓰레기들의 돈을 뜯어 목구멍을 채우겠다고 아랫도리를 내놓는 여자들은 더 말할 것이 없었다. 그런 여자들과 아무리 많이 몸을 섞는다해도 그 누구 하나 순임이 같은 말을 할 리가 없었다.

실로 너무나 오랜만에 만석은 자신의 장래를 생각해 주는 정이 담긴 말을 들은 것이었다. 그것도 술집 작부나 창녀가 아닌 여자한테서 말이다. 만석은 무일푼이라는 것도 잊어버렸다. 마흔아홉이라는 나이도 잊어버렸다. 그저 벅차고 두근거리는 마음의 갈피를 잡을 수가 없는 채로 전과는 달리 일이 힘드는 줄을 몰랐다.

"나도 잘 모르겠어요. 그냥 마음이……."

국밥집에 드나드는 공사판 사람들 중에 다른 젊은것들도 많은데 왜 하필이면 나이 많은 자기냐고 묻는 말에 순

time to time, when such thoughts threatened to overpower him, he would simply drink himself into a deathlike stupor.

Over the past thirty years, wandering from place to place in search of work, he had known countless women. They were encounters that had nothing to do with love; they had been the purchase of services. After all, if manual laborers are human trash, then what can be said about the women who eat by selling themselves to such trash? No matter how often one mixed one's flesh with such women, not a single one of them would ever have spoken as Sun-im had.

Indeed, it had been ages since anyone had expressed such affectionate concern about his future. And the words had come from a woman who was neither a bargirl nor a whore. Man-sŏk forgot his penniless condition. He even forgot the fact that he was forty-nine years old. With his heart full and his mind distracted, even his work no longer seemed as burdensome.

"I'm not sure myself, it's just that my heart feels..."

When he asked Sun-im why she was concerned about him, of all the men who frequented the canteen, she blushed and couldn't reply.

임이는 얼굴을 붉히며 이렇게 말꼬리를 흐리고 말았다.

"내 나이 마흔아홉, 임자 나이 서른셋이면 몇 살 간격인지나 아는가?"

"진시황은 하룻밤을 자려고 만리성을 쌓았대요."

순임이는 아주 유식하게 대답했다.

"허, 참……."

만석은 더 할 말이 없었다.

만석은 순임이의 말을 듣고 욕심껏 계산을 해 나가기 시작했다. 자기를 닮은 자식을 키워 보고 싶었다. 술을 바짝 줄이고 사 먹는 밥값만 모으면 너끈히 살림을 꾸려 갈 수 있을 것이었다. 허리끈 조이고 알뜰살뜰 살면 한곳에 뿌리내리고 떠돌이 신세도 면하게 될 것이다. 사람답게 한번 살아 보라고 하늘이 점지해 준 짝이라 싶었다.

막노동으로 시달린 마흔아홉 살의 육신이 갑자기 새순 돋는 봄나무처럼 싱싱해지는 것을 느꼈다. 항시 희뿌연 구름으로 덮여 있던 마음도 가을 하늘처럼 활짝 개어 있었다. 매일이다시피 마시던 술을 거의 입에 대지 않았다. 굳이 마다했던 야간작업에도 나섰다. 그래도 노곤한 줄을 몰랐다. 점례를 색시로 맞아들이기 위해 뼈 휘는 줄 모르고 일을 했던 스무 살 적 근력이 되살아난 것 같았다.

"I'm forty-nine, you're thirty-three, do you realize what that will mean?"

"They say the Qin Emperor built the Great Wall of China for one night of pleasure," Sun-im replied.

"Ah, well."

Man-sŏk had no reply to Sun-im's clever words, but on his own, he eagerly began to calculate. He wanted a child of his own. By drastically cutting his spending for meals and liquor, he thought he could save enough to support a family. If he worked hard enough, he might even be able to put down roots in one place and stop drifting around. The woman began to seem like a godsend, at long last an actual chance to live like a human being.

His body of forty-nine years, worn down by manual work, suddenly began to feel like a budding tree in springtime. His mind, too, always so clouded until then, cleared like an autumn sky. The liquor he had come to drink daily now remained scarcely touched. He even volunteered for the night-shift, something he never used to do—and still, fatigue couldn't touch him. It was as if he had regained the strength of his twenties, of the days when he had worked to win Jŏm-rye as his bride.

After three months of this tireless work, he man-

석 달을 그렇게 악다구니로 보내고 나니 수중에는 제법 목돈이 잡혔다.

"인자 사글세방 하나 장만헐 액수는 모아졌는갑구만."

만석은 순임이 앞에서 고개도 제대로 못 들고 이렇게 말했다.

"어머, 벌써요? 내가 사람 한번 틀림없이 봤군요. 젊은 것들로는 어림도 없는 일예요. 이런 날을 얼마나 기다렸다구요."

순임이는 생각했던 것보다 훨씬 더 반가워하고 기뻐했다.

혼례식이고 뭐고 필요한 게 아니었다. 방 하나를 얻어 살림을 차렸다.

"서른 계집 암내에 쉰 사내 기둥뿌리 빠질 테니 조심해."

"암, 암, 스물 계집 고게 비지살 조개라면 서른 계집 고건 찰고무 조개야. 선불리 꺼떡대다간 허리까지 내려앉는다구."

노동판 험한 입들은 만석의 느닷없는 색시 맞이를 그대로 보고 넘기지 않았다.

"요런 버르장머리 읎는 삭신들아, 염려들 말어. 안즉 아

aged to save a significant sum.

"I think I have enough cash now to rent a room," Man-sŏk told Sun-im one day, too diffident to look her in the eye.

"My goodness, already? I sure picked out the right man. A young man never could have done it. I've been waiting for this day so long!"

Sun-im's delight surpassed his expectations.

A formal wedding seemed unnecessary. They rented a room and set up a household together.

"Take care, the fire of a thirty-year-old woman might burn up a fifty-year-old root."

"Sure, sure, a twenty-year-old's clam is mushy, but a thirty-year-old's is like rubber. If you don't watch out your things will go, too."

His filthy-minded coworkers couldn't let Man-sŏk's abrupt betrothal pass by without comment.

"Don't worry, you low-lives, I still have power enough to sire ten sons," Man-sŏk retorted with unusual good humor.

And Man-sŏk was utterly satisfied. His long and aimless ordeal had come to an end. A glimmer of hope now shone above what had been the gloomy horizon of his future. Where before he had resigned himself to the fact that man enters the world empty-

들로만 열은 뽑을 기운이 남았응께.”

만석은 주책없다 싶게 벙글거리며 맞받아 넘겼다.

사실 만석은 더없는 행복감에 취해 있었다. 길고 긴 떠돌이 생활이 일단은 끝을 맺은 것이다. 그리고 암울하고 한심스럽던 앞날에 어렴풋이 희망이 보이기 시작한 것이다. 맨주먹으로 왔다가 맨주먹으로 가는 것이 사람의 한 평생이라고 체념하고 살았었다. 그러나 그건 어디까지나 답답했던 때의 생각이었다. 한번쯤은 사람답게 살아 보고 싶은 욕심은 언제나 마음 깊은 곳에 도사리고 있었던 것이다.

신방 아닌 신방을 차렸던 날 밤, 만석의 가슴에는 지나간 세월의 기억들이 슬픔과 아픔으로 되살아나고 있었다.

“말씨로 고향이 전라도라는 건 아는데 장가는 첨 드는 건가요?”

신방치레를 한차례 치르고 나서 순임이가 물은 말이었다.

“첨이면 어떻고 열 번, 스무 번째면 워쩔 것잉가?”

만석은 퉁명스럽게 되물었다. 그러면서 딴 생각에 깊이 빠져들고 있었다.

“어쩌긴요? 이제 부부가 됐으니 이런저런 것들이 궁금해서 그러지요.”

handed and leaves in the same condition, such thoughts became a thing of the past, back when he had had no future to live for. Somewhere deep in his soul, there had always been a desire to live for once like a human being.

On their first night together, all the aching memories of his past resurfaced and filled his heart.

"I can tell you're from Chŏlla Province—it's your accent. Is this your first marriage, then?"

This was Sun-im's first question after consummating their newly formed bond.

"What does it matter whether this is the first, or the tenth, or the twentieth?" Man-sŏk replied shortly, his mind elsewhere.

"What do you mean? Now that we're husband and wife, I'm naturally a little curious about this and that."

"Curiosity killed the cat. I have no wife nor children left behind, so don't be fretting about the past. The future is what we need to be planning for."

"Still, there are things I ought to know, like where you were born, why you've been leading the life of a vagabond, and where your parents and relatives live."

"Oh, shut up!"

"굼벵이를 삶아 묵었능가. 궁금허게. 따로 챙개 논 처자석 읎응께 임자는 쓰잘데읎는 생각 말고 앞으로 살 일이나 궁리허드라고."

"그래도 고향이 어딘지, 왜 떠돌며 살게 됐는지, 부모님 형제간은 어디 사는지, 알아야 될 게 있잖아요."

"아, 시끄러!"

만석은 눈을 부릅뜨며 벌떡 일어나 앉았다. 그런 그의 눈은 섬뜩한 살기를 품고 있었다.

"니가 면서기여, 지서 순사여. 워디다 써 묵자고 쓰잘데읎는 과거지사를 꼬치꼬치 캐고 야단이여. 니나 나나 오다가다 눈 맞고 배 맞어 어디 한번 살아 보자는 것뿐인디 멋헌다고 과거지사는 캐고 지랄이여. 오지기 내놀 것 읎고, 보잘것읎으먼 뜬구름맹키로 떠돌이 신세가 됐을 것잉가. 나는 족보도 읎고 고향도 읎는 진짜배기 상것이니께 고런 것 따지고 살라먼 당장 짐 싸갖고 나가 뿌러. 아, 싸게 나가랑께!"

만석은 곧 후려칠 것처럼 벌겋게 흥분되어 있었다.

"아녜요, 그게 아녜요. 난 관심을 써 준다고 생각하고 한 말인데…… 잘못했어요. 다시는 안 물을게요."

한바탕 날벼락을 맞고 난 마누라 순임이는 돌아누워 깊

Man-sŏk sat up abruptly and glared at her. There was a murderous glint in his eyes.

"What are you, a detective or a government clerk? Why do you need to interrogate me about my past? You and I just happened to cross paths and to hook up, so what's the point in digging up ancient history? You don't become an aimless drifter if your past life gives you anything worth bragging about. I have no pedigree, no home, and I come from the lowest stock, so if you want to poke and pry into such things you might as well pack up and go right now. Just leave if you want!"

Man-sŏk grew red with ire, coming close to striking her.

"No, no, it wasn't that at all. I was just asking to show that I care about you... It was my fault. I'll never ask again."

Thunderstruck by his reaction, his wife rolled over, turning her back. Looking at her skinny shoulders, Man-sŏk felt sorry for her. She was right, all she had done was to ask some ordinary questions about her new husband; he had greatly overreacted. Still, it couldn't be helped. It was his past that had forced him to live like a fugitive criminal for thirty long years. His life had been no better than death

은 잠에 빠져 있었다. 만석은 그녀의 가난한 어깨를 물끄러미 바라보며 미안하다고 생각했다. 그녀의 말마따나 새로 맞은 남편에 대한 예의로 물었을 뿐인 말을 가지고 자신이 너무 지나치게 흥분한 것이었다. 그러나 그건 어쩔 수 없는 일이었다. 그 과거라는 것 때문에 삼십 년 가까이나 죄인으로 숨어 다니고 쫓기며 살아온 것이었다. 그동안 살아 있었다고는 하지만 죽은 것이나 뭐가 달랐던가. 세월이 많이 달라졌다고는 하지만 지금까지도 고향엘 갈 수가 없는 것은 자신의 죄가 그대로 남아 있는 증거였다. 정씨 문중이 그대로 자리 잡고 있는 고향에 내려가면 그들은 당장 자신을 생매장하고 말 것이었다. 어제까지 한편이었던 인민군의 총질에 쫓겨 초저녁 어스름을 타고 고향을 도망쳐 나온 후로 그 누구에게도 입을 열지 않던 과거였다.

"개잡년!"

만석은 부르르 치를 떨었다. 그 생각만 하면 전신이 싸늘하게 굳어지며 피가 머리로 뻗쳤다. 그리고 그때의 장면들이 세월의 흐름과는 상관없이 한 치도 틀리지 않고 되살아나는 것이었다. 원래 기억력이 좋은 편이 못 되었고, 마흔 고개를 넘기면서부터는 며칠 전 일도 까맣게 잊

that whole time. Though the times had greatly changed, the fact that he could never go back to his hometown was proof that nothing could be done to undo his crime. If ever he returned there, to the land where the Chŏng clan still lived, they would instantly bury him alive. It was a past he had never divulged to a soul, not since the hour he had fled from his hometown with the People's Army on his heels, pursued by men who only a day before had been his comrades.

"The filthy bitch!"

Man-sŏk trembled all over. The mere thought of it made his whole body stiffen and all the blood in his body rushed to his head. It had all been so long ago, but each moment came back vividly into his imagination. His memory had never been particularly good, and since turning forty he sometimes had trouble recalling events just a few days old, but those few scenes had been indelibly imprinted on his mind by some strange process. Even photographs lose their color after three decades, but not these memories. These retained not only their original colors but even their very smells.

"The bitch should've been drawn and quartered!"

Man-sŏk shut his eyes and exhaled a fiery breath.

어먹고 하는데, 그때의 기억만큼은 어쩌면 그리도 생생하게 박혀 있는지 모를 일이었다. 사진도 삼십 년 세월이면 누렇게 변색하게 마련인데 그 기억만은 전혀 변색할 줄을 몰랐다. 모습이 변색을 하지 않은 것만 아니라 장면 장면에 따라 그때의 냄새까지 역력하게 맡아지는 것은 또 어찌된 일인가.

"육시헐 년!"

만석은 눈을 질끈 감으며 뜨거운 숨을 토해 냈다.

점례 그년이 옷만 홀랑 벗고 있지 않았더라도 그년까지 죽이지는 않았을 것이다. 아랫도리만 벗겨져 있었더라면 그놈한테 당한 일이라고 덮어 버릴 수도 있었다. 그런데 새끼까지 배고 있던 년이 옷을 홀랑 벗어던지고 그놈과 엉클어져 있었던 것이다.

인민위원회 부위원장 만석은 시(市)인민위원회에 보고 사항을 가지고 이틀 간 집을 비워야 했다. 부하 두 명을 대동한 행차는 만석의 기분을 더없이 들뜨게 만들었다.

"천 동무, 동무의 혁명 투쟁은 혁혁한 것이오. 동무의 위원장 임명은 시간문제요. 잘 다녀오도록 하오."

길을 떠나기 직전에 했던 분주소장의 목소리가 귓가에 쟁쟁했다. 위원장이 되면…… 만석은 옆에서 걷고 있는

If only she hadn't been totally naked, perhaps he'd have let her live. If she had just been nude from the waist down, he would have assumed that she was being raped. But the bitch, child in her belly, hadn't had a stitch on. And she'd been clinging to that bastard in ecstasy.

Man-sŏk, then Deputy Chairman of the local People's Committee, had needed to be away for two days to confer with the People's Council in the city. That he was accompanied on this journey by two aides greatly fed his pride.

"Comrade Ch'ŏn, your service to the revolutionary cause has been brilliant. It is only a matter of time until you attain the rank of Chairman. Have a good trip back."

The voice of the People's Army commander at the hour of his departure was still ringing in his ears. When I become Chairman... Man-sŏk clenched his fists without attracting the attention of his two companions. Even at the rank of Deputy Chairman, the power he had been able to exercise was already beyond belief. It was a power that had enabled him to wreak revenge for all the hunger he had suffered over his twenty-five years. And now, once he

두 부하가 모르게 주먹을 말아 쥐었다. 부위원장이라는 자리만으로 그동안 휘둘러 온 권한은 스스로 믿어지지 않을 정도였다. 이십오 년 세월 동안 겪어 왔던 배고픔과 서러움을 한풀이하기에 부족함이 없었다. 그런데 위원장이 되면…… 두말할 것도 없이 감골·학내·죽촌 마을이 다 자신의 것이 되는 것이다.

사실 위원장을 맡고 있는 수길은 못마땅한 데가 한두 가지가 아니었다. 곧잘 나가다가도 엉거주춤 겁을 먹거나 망설일 때가 있었다. 수길이 위원장 자리에 앉혀진 것은 순전히 나이를 세 살 더 먹었다는 것뿐이었다.

정참봉네 큰손자를 처형할 때도 수길은 등신처럼 머뭇거렸다. 서울에서 법을 공부하던 그가 마을에 잠입했다는 소문이 돌았다. 바로 정참봉네 식구들을 끌어다가 요절을 내 버릴 수도 있었지만 일단 비밀 수색을 하기로 했다. 얼마 전에 읍장을 지내던 정참봉 아들이 처형되어 집안이 쑥밭이 되었기 때문이었다. 나흘을 잠복한 끝에 정참봉네 손자는 당숙 집의 대밭 토굴에서 체포됐던 것이다.

그는 뒷등 소나무 아래로 끌려 나갔고, 갈 길은 빤히 정해져 있었다. 그는 파리한 얼굴에 입을 꼭 다문 채로 이쪽을 뚫어지게 쏘아보고 있었다.

became Chairman... Kamgol, Hangnae, Jukch'on—those villages would all doubtlessly be under his control.

As a matter of fact, the conduct of Su-gil, the present Chairman, had been unsatisfactory in more than a few respects. While ordinarily his orders were all right, at times he wavered or grew frightened. The only reason he, instead of Man-sŏk, had been installed as Chairman in the first place, was that he was three years older.

When the time came to execute the eldest grandson of the Chŏng landlord clan, Su-gil, like an imbecile, had hesitated. According to rumor, the grandson, who was then studying law in Seoul, had secretly returned and stolen his way back into the village. It would have been possible to round up the Chŏngs and coerce the information out of them, but instead Su-gil began with a quiet search. Not long before, the student's father, the eldest son of the family and mayor of the town, had been executed, and the entire Chŏng clan was already in dire straits. After four days of close surveillance, the People's Army finally trapped the grandson in a cellar dug beneath a bamboo field owned by one of his cousins.

"엄니 초상에 쌀 한 말을 내준 것이 바로 저 형규였어."

수길이 떨리는 목소리로 나직하게 한 말이었다.

"그려서, 살려 주자 그런 말이당가요?"

만석은 잠시의 틈도 주지 않고 대질렀다.

"멋이냐, 꼭 그러잔 것이 아니라……."

"위원장 동무, 혁명 완수를 위해서는 과감허게……."

일부러 목청을 돋우어 분주소장의 말을 흉내 내는데, 이상한 낌새를 챘는지 뒤에 서 있던 분주소장이 다가서며 물었다.

"뭣들 하는 게요?"

순간 수길의 얼굴이 굳어지면서 만석을 애원하듯 바라보았다.

"저 반동을 얼렁 처단해 뿔자고 헌 말이구만이라."

만석은 재빨리 대꾸했다. 그러면서, 살았다 싶게 어깨를 늘어뜨리는 수길의 모습을 지켜보았다.

"좋소, 빨리 처단하시오!"

분주소장의 명령이 떨어지자 만석은 대창을 들고 서 있는 부하들에게 눈짓했다. 세 명은 대창을 꼬나 잡고 소나무에 묶여 있는 정참봉네 손자를 향하여 돌진했다. 그리고 온 산을 찢고, 하늘을 찢고, 땅까지 찢어발기는 것 같은

He was taken out to a hillside and there, under a pine tree, his fate was decided. His face pale and his lips closed tightly, he stared at his captors, his gaze piercing.

"This is the same Chŏng Hyŏng-gyu who gave us a pig to roast at my mother's funeral," said Su-gil in a low, trembling voice.

"So are you saying his life should be spared?" Man-sŏk snapped at him.

"Well, not exactly, but..."

"Comrade Chairman, for the sake of the revolution one must courageously..."

As Man-sŏk began to raise his voice in deliberate imitation of the People's Army commander, that same commander sensed from a distance that something was amiss and started over towards them.

"What's going on here?" he asked.

At that instant Su-gil's features froze into an imploring look aimed at Man-sŏk.

"We were just saying that this reactionary element should be executed forthwith," Man-sŏk hastily replied. As he spoke, he noticed Su-gil's shoulders droop with relief.

"Good! Hurry and get rid of him."

At the commander's order, Man-sŏk signaled to his

비명 소리가 길게 길게 퍼져나가고 있었다. 그때 수길은 눈을 꼭 감은 채 나무토막처럼 뻣뻣이 굳어져 서 있었다. 그런 수길을 비웃음으로 바라보고 서 있는 만석은, 네놈은 위원장 자격이 없어, 생각하고 있었다.

만석은 수길과 반대로 그 길게 퍼져나가는 비명 소리를 들으며 전신 마디마디가 짜릿짜릿해지는 쾌감을 느끼고 있었다. 그 쾌감은 곧 복수심이었다. 대대로 종놈으로 살아왔고, 태어나서 지금까지 스물다섯 해 동안 겪어 온 모든 서러움과 고통과 억울함이 그 짜릿짜릿한 쾌감 속에서 천천히 천천히 씻겨 나가고 있었다. 만석은 그 쾌감이 마누라 점례 위에서 느끼는 쾌감보다 더 뜨겁고 진하고 아찔아찔하게 느껴졌다. 마누래 배 위에서 느끼는 쾌감도 환장할 만한 것이긴 했지만 그건 너무나 짧았고, 그리고 금방 낭떠러지로 떨어지는 것 같은 허망함이 찬 기운으로 몰려드는 것이었다. 그러나 자신을 사람 취급하지 않았던 자들의 마지막 비명 소리에서 느끼는 쾌감은 잊을 수 없는 기억들이 줄지어 떠오르다 사라지는 시간만큼 길었고, 아쉬움은 있을망정 낭떠러지로 떨어지는 것 같은 허망함은 없었다.

머잖아 위원장이 되리라는 기대에 부풀어 시위원회에

men, who stood nearby holding bamboo spears. The three men lunged their spears into the Chŏng family's grandson, who was tied to the pine tree. The horrible scream that echoed forth seemed to tear at the fabric of the sky and shake the hill itself. Su-gil stood as stiff as a board with his eyes tightly shut. Watching Su-gil, Man-sŏk sneered and told himself that the man was unfit for the office of Chairman.

Unlike Su-gil, Man-sŏk felt a tingle of pleasure in his bones as he listened to the shrieks of pain. It was the pleasure of vengeance. The suffering of generations of slaves, of his own travails over the twenty-five years since his birth—it was all slowly being washed away by that wave of pleasure. The satisfaction bestowed by it was hotter, denser and more dazzling than that he received from his wife. To be atop his wife drove him insane with pleasure, but it was all too brief and afterwards he always felt as if he'd fallen from a cliff. This pleasure at the screaming endured as long as the memories of injustice kept recurring; it was not quite perfect, perhaps, but it lacked the emptiness of the other sensation.

When he arrived in the city to meet with the

도착했고, 거기서 내리는 급한 지시 사항을 가지고 당일로 오십 리 길을 되돌아와야 했다.

위원회 사무실에 당도했을 때는 해가 뉘엿뉘엿했다. 긴 여름 하루 종일 백 리 길을 걷느라고 만석은 지칠 대로 지쳐 있었다. 사무실에는 아무도 없었다. 우선 두 부하를 돌려보냈다. 지시 사항을 전달하기 위해서 자신은 분주소장을 만나야 했다. 다리를 책상 위에 올려놓고 한동안 앉아 있던 만석은 언뜻 이상하다는 생각을 했다. 사무실이 이렇게 텅 비어 있을 리가 없었다. 무슨 큰일이 일어나지 않고서는 있을 수 없는 일이었다. 이대로 앉아만 있을 게 아니라 찾아봐야겠다는 생각을 했다.

사무실을 나온 만석은 뒤로 붙어 있는 숙소로 돌아갔다. 숙소에 누가 있나 싶어서였다.

숙소로 가까이 다가가던 만석은 무의식적으로 걸음을 멈추었다. 이상한 느낌의 인기척이 새어나왔던 것이다. 다시 귀를 기울였다. 그건 분명 밤일을 할 때나 내는 남녀의 소리였다. 순간 만석은 속이 꿈틀 꼬이는 것 같은 야릇한 기분으로 긴장했다. 그리고 자신도 모르게 좌우를 빠르게 살폈다. 어떤 황소 뱃가죽 가진 놈이 벌건 대낮에 위원회 숙소에서…… 이런 생각과 함께 몸은 벌써 창가로

Council, he fully anticipated that he would be made a Chairman. Instead, he was given urgent orders, and found himself unexpectedly traversing the fifty *li* back home on the same day.

It was nearing dusk by the time he returned and made his way back up to the local People's Committee office. By then, having walked a hundred *li* on a summer day, Man-sŏk was exhausted to the marrow. Nobody was in the office. He sent his two aides home. In order to deliver his urgent communication, he had to talk with the Chairman himself. After a few minutes of sitting with his feet propped up on the desk, a strange thought occurred to him. It was most unusual for the office to be unoccupied like this. That only happened in cases of real emergency. Rather than just sit there waiting, he decided to go out and investigate the cause.

Leaving the office, he went around the corner to the nearby barracks, where the staff slept. He intended to see if anybody there could tell him what was going on.

As he approached the barracks, Man-sŏk stopped short. An odd sort of sound was coming from inside. He listened again as it continued. It was undoubtedly the sound of a man and woman in

찰싹 달라붙어 있었다.

"어, 어……."

만석은 그만 소리를 지를 뻔했다. 엎어져 있는 사내놈의 얼굴은 저쪽으로 돌려져 파묻혀 있었기 때문에 알 수가 없었지만, 눈을 꼬옥 감은 채 입을 반쯤 벌리고 끙끙대고 누워 있는 건 바로 자신의 마누라 점례였던 것이다.

만석은 머리가 핑그르르 돌며 앞이 캄캄해지는 걸 느꼈다. 그리고 다음 순간 전신에 불이 붙는 것 같은 뜨거움이 뱃속에서 터져 올랐다.

눈에 보이는 대로 커다란 돌을 집어 들었다. 그리고 문을 박차고 들었다.

"요런 개잡녀러 것들아!"

엎어져 있던 사내가 딱 굳어지는 것 같더니 벌떡 일어섰다. 그 순간 커다란 돌덩이가 사내의 뒤통수에 퍽 소리를 내며 떨어졌다. 벌거벗은 사내의 몸뚱어리는 괴상하게 짧은 비명을 토하며 그대로 방바닥에 뒹굴어졌다. 거의 동시에 알몸의 여자는 발딱 일어나 두 팔로 가슴을 가린 채 파랗게 질려 앉은걸음으로 방구석을 향해 쫓기고 있었다. 눈에 불을 켜고 이빨을 앙다문 만석이 다가서고 있었던 것이다. 여자는 마침내 방구석에 막혀 더는 뒤로 물러

nocturnal embrace. Instantly, he grew tense, filled with an eerie sense of foreboding. Swiftly, he spun around and looked to see if anyone was about. What kind of a thick-skinned bastard would have the nerve to do it in the Committee barracks in broad daylight.... Before he knew it, his face was cemented to the windowpane.

"Ah, ah..." He almost screamed out loud.

He couldn't make out the bastard's face since it was buried, but the woman, moaning through a mouth half agape, her eyes shut, was none other than his wife.

Man-sŏk became dizzy and his vision went black. He caught fire, a burning lump bursting inside him. Without thinking, he knelt down and picked up a big stone. He kicked the door in, shouting.

"You filthy animals!"

The prone man grew rigid and instantly scrambled to his feet just as the large rock struck the back of his skull with a dull thud. The naked man emitted a brief cry and crumpled onto the floor. Almost simultaneously, the nude woman sat up, covering her breasts with crossed arms, and scrambled on her knees toward the corner. She was as white as a sheet. Man-sŏk came after her, his teeth clenched

날 수 없게 되었고, 발가벗은 몸은 방구석에서 와들와들 떨며 점점 조그맣게 오그라들고 있었다. 만석은 짐승처럼 다가서고 있었다. 한 발짝 앞까지 만석이 다가섰을 때였다.

"살려 주씨요오."

소리를 지르며 여자가 몸을 튕겨 앞으로 내달았다. 그 때 만석의 발길이 여자의 배를 걷어찼다. 여자는 돌로 뒤통수를 맞은 사내처럼 짧은 비명을 토하며 방바닥에 나뒹굴었다.

만석은 이빨을 뿌드득 갈아붙이며 사내 쪽으로 돌아섰다. 사내는 머리에서 피를 철철 쏟으며 꿈지럭거리고 있었다. 허공에 뻗쳐진 사내의 팔은 푸들푸들 경련을 일으키고 있었다. 한사코 무언가를 잡으려는 몸짓이었다. 만석은 엎어진 사내의 얼굴을 발로 차서 돌렸다.

"아니! 니놈이……."

만석은 섬뜩 물러섰다. 그 사내는 분주소장이었다. 그렇게 하늘처럼 믿었던 분주소장이……. 속았다는 분노가 창 밖에서 마누라의 얼굴을 확인했을 때보다 더 뜨겁게 전신을 터져 나왔다.

거의 흰창뿐인 눈을 홉뜬 분주소장은 여전히 허공으로 팔을 뻗친 채 몸을 꿈틀대고 있었다. 그 팔을 뻗친 방향에

and ire in his eyes. She had no avenue of escape; all she could do was sit, naked, trambling in the corner. He kept moving towards her, his pace like a predatory animal. Only one step separated them.

"Don't kill me, please!"

As she shrieked for mercy, she tried to spring away and escape. Man-sŏk kicked her in the stomach. Like the man before her, she also gave a short cry and rolled down onto the floor.

Grinding his teeth, Man-sŏk turned back toward the man. He was squirming on the floor as blood gushed forth from his head. His arms flailed wildly, as if he were trying to grasp at the air itself. Man-sŏk kicked his face up with his boot to see if he could recognize him.

"Why... it's you, you bastard!"

Startled, Man-sŏk retreated a step. It was the People's Army commander. He had guessed the man was from the People's Army, but never imagined it could have been the commander himself. The commander he had worshiped like a god. His rage at this breach of trust was even greater than what he had felt at recognizing his wife's face from the window.

The commander was still squirming and flailing

따발총이 놓여 있었다. 만석은 따발총을 집어 들었다. 그리고 사내의 하복부를 향해 방아쇠를 당겼다.

따따따따…….

만석은 마누라 쪽으로 돌아섰다. 마누라는 그사이 몸을 가누어 일어나선 문 쪽으로 엉금엉금 기어가고 있었다. 만석의 눈앞에 커다란 마누라의 둔부가 확대되어 왔다. 두 엉덩이 사이에 그대로 노출된 그것은 돼지의 그것처럼 더럽고 추악했다. 만석은 그곳을 향해 다시 방아쇠를 당겼다.

따따따따…….

탄환이 더 나가지 않게 되었을 때 만석은 총을 내던졌다. 방 안은 피바다가 되었고, 그 속에 내장이 터져 나온 두 시체는 나자빠져 있었다.

만석은 도망가야 된다고 생각하며 황급히 숙소를 뛰쳐나왔다. 그리고 산길 쪽을 향해 내닫기 시작했다.

"시상은 참아 감서 살아야 허는 것이여. 한을 험허게 풀면 또 다른 한이 태이는 것이여. 안 되야, 안 되야, 지발 사람 상허게 말어."

아버지의 음성이 줄곧 따라오고 있었다. 어머니의 찌든 얼굴이 어른거렸다. 세 살 먹은 아들이 방싯거리며 "아부

his arms, his eyes rolling back in his head. He was struggling to reach a machine gun that lay not far away. Man-sŏk picked up the weapon and fired it, aiming below the belt.

Ta-ta-ta-ta-ta...

Man-sŏk turned again to his wife. She had managed to pull herself to her knees again and was crawling in the direction of the door. From where he stood, his wife's rear end loomed before him as if magnified. What he saw was as loathsome as a sow's bottom. Man-sŏk pulled the trigger again, aiming right at it.

Ta-ta-ta-ta-ta...

When the weapon was emptied of bullets, Man-sŏk threw it aside. The room was like a sea of blood, intestines spilling out from the ripped up corpses.

Suddenly aware that he had better leave, Man-sŏk rushed out of the barracks. He took off, running toward the mountain trail.

"You must lead the life for which you were born. Who do you think you are? What made you think you could murder people like they were dogs? It's wrong, wrong, and heaven will punish you for it."

His father's voice pursued him as he ran. Before

지, 아부지" 부르고 있었다.

새 마누라 순임이는 다시는 지난 이야기를 묻는 일 없이 그런대로 살림을 꾸려 나갔다. 만석은 사는 재미가 이런 것인가, 새삼스럽게 느끼며 아직도 젊은 마누라를 품고 전과는 다른 온기 서린 잠을 깊이 잘 수 있었다.

공사판 저쪽 멀리로 아지랑이가 간지럼을 타듯 아롱거리고, 아파트도 예정대로 다 되어 가고 있을 무렵이었다.

"몸이 영 이상해요."

마누라가 눈을 내리깔고 한 말이었다.

"멋을 잘못 묵었간디?"

만석은, 물약이나 한 병 사다 묵어 하는 식으로 말하고 말았다.

"그게 아니구요, 꽃이 두 달째나 안 비쳐요."

"꽃……?"

되물어 놓고는 만석은 머릿속에 전등불이 환하게 켜지는 걸 느꼈다.

"워메, 소식이 있단 말이당가?"

만석은 들뜬 목소리로 물었고,

"그렇당께요."

his eyes floated the weary visage of his mother. He heard his three-year-old son calling him in a sweet tone, “Da-da, da-da.”

His new wife Sun-im, who never again asked about his past, gave him a decent family life. Man-sŏk felt life was worth living at last; he could actually sleep soundly with his young wife in his arms.

By this time the hot air danced and shimmered over the concrete of the construction site, and the buildings were going to be finished on schedule.

“I’m feeling very queer,” his wife said, her eyes lowered.

“Eaten something bad?” Man-sŏk replied, as if to suggest she take some digestive tonic.

“No, it’s not that; for two months I’ve had no sign of a flower.”

“Flower?”

Repeating the word, a bright light went on in Man-sŏk’s brain.

“What? You mean there’s news!’

“That’s what I mean,” his wife answered, apparently embarrassed.

“You just go ahead and drop me a son—I’ll work twice as hard, and you’ll live a life of luxury,” Man-sŏk said, grabbing her by the hand.

마누라는 만석의 말을 흉내 내며 부끄러운 듯 눈을 흘겼다.

"아들 하나만 쑥 빼내 뿔소. 나가 곱절로 일을 혀서 호강시킬 팅께."

만석은 마누라의 손을 덥석 잡으며 말했고,

"징그러워요. 낳지 어떻게 빼내요."

마누라는 수줍게 웃었다.

"평생을 있는 놈덜 발밑에 밟히고 사는 쌍놈 신센 줄 알았으면 자식새끼는 애시당초 낳지를 말았어야제라. 요런 세상 불거지지 않았으면 머 땀새 요런 드러운 꼴 당했을랍디여."

"지멋대로 뚫어진 구멍이라고 저놈 말허는 것 잠 보소. 니놈이 그 나이에 멀 알 것이냐. 이담에 나이 들면 다 지절로 알게 될 팅께."

아버지는 열여덟 살의 만석이를 더는 탓하지 않았었다.

스물한 살에 장가를 든 것도 꼭 마음이 내켰던 것은 아니었다. 부모들의 성화에는 아예 관심도 없었고, 장난삼아 색싯감을 얼핏 보았는데 그 인물이 아주 잘생겼던 것이다. 상것 취급을 받기엔 너무 아깝게 잘생긴 얼굴이었다. 그래서 마지못한 것처럼 장가를 들었고, 잠자리를 함

"Oh, don't be so vulgar," she said with a coy grin.

"If you, born a slave, knew you'd remain a nobody, ground under the heels of the rich for your whole life, you never should've brought offspring into the world. And if I'd never been born your son, I never would've had to swallow all this sickening abuse."

"Listen to you! You think just because there's a hole in your face you deserve to be heard. What do you know at your age? You'll learn, when you've lived in this world awhile."

Man-sŏk's father had no more severe reproach than this for his impertinent eighteen-year-old son.

When Man-sŏk married at twenty-one, it wasn't exactly what he wanted to do. His parents' urgings to wed had left him cold, but when the time came, the bride arranged for him turned out to be quite pretty—far too beautiful to live the hard life of a peasant. And so he married her with feigned reluctance, and, sharing a bed with her, soon became a father. Yet, even then, he still didn't understand what his father had tried to tell him. Or, rather, his father's admonitions were simply forgotten, cleanly erased from his mind.

So why now, at the age of fifty, had his father's

께하다 보니 애아버지가 된 것이었다. 그때도 아버지의 말뜻이 무엇이었는지 깨닫지를 못했다. 아니, 아버지의 말은 아예 생각나지도 않았다.

그런데 쉰의 나이에 마누라의 임신 소식을 들으며 삼십이 년 전의 아버지 말이 떠오르는 것은 무슨 까닭인가. 아버지의 말대로 나이가 들어서 저절로 알게 된 것인가. 이 세상에서 한평생을 살다 가며 제 핏줄을 남긴다는 것은 말로 다 헤아릴 수 없는 어떤 깊은 뜻이 있다는 것을 만석은 어렴풋이 느끼고 있었다.

마누라의 배가 차츰 불러 오기 시작하면서 공사판의 일도 다 끝나 가고 있었다. 마누라는 공사판을 찾아 떠돌아야 한다는 사실을 무서워했다. 그래서 취직자리를 알아보겠다고 나섰다.

“아, 시장시런 소리 하덜 말어. 배워 묵은 것이라곤 농새짓는 것허고 노동판 품팔이뿐인디 취직은 무신 놈에 취직이여.”

만석은 처음부터 만류했지만 마누라는 듣지 않았다. 마누라가 며칠 만에 알아 온 것이 공단의 경비직이었다. 밤에만 일을 해야 하는 그 자리마저도 만석의 처음 예상대로 자격 미달이었다. 중졸 이상으로 제한한 학벌이 그랬

words returned to him the moment he learned of his new wife's pregnancy? Perhaps he was finally old and experienced enough to realize what his father had been trying to tell him so many years before. Man-sŏk could begin to understand now the unfathomable truth of the instinct that drives a man to leave behind his own flesh and blood.

As Man-sŏk's wife's belly continued to swell, the construction job drew to a close. Dreading the prospect of drifting about in search of new work, she proposed to go out on her own to try and line up a steady job for him.

"Don't spout such nonsense. The only skills I've ever learned are fanning and menial construction work. What sort of steady job can I get?"

Man-sŏk was opposed to the idea from the start, but his wife refused to take no far an answer. After several days, she came back home to tell him of a possible position as a security guard at an industrial complex. The work would have been at night, but, as Man-sŏk had expected, he did not meet the qualifications in any case. The job called for at least a middle-school education, applicants under thirty-five were preferred, and a personal reference was required. He was able to meet none of these pre-

고, 서른다섯 이하로 못 박은 나이가 그랬고, 재정 보증인, 신원 조회, 자격 미달은 한두 가지가 아니었다. 마누라는 두어 군데 더 알아보고 나서는 포기했다.

"내가 다시 국밥집에 나가 일을 했으면 했지 떠돌이 신세로는 못 살아요."

"멋이 워쩌고 워째? 나허고 배맞춤시롱 여그서 죽을 때꺼정 살라고 작정혔더란 것이여?"

다시 국밥집에 나간다는 말에 만석은 그만 화가 머리꼭지로 치솟았다.

"귀때기 활짝 열고 내 말 똑똑허니 들어. 다리몽댕이 뿐질러 뿔기 전에 방구석에 달싹 말고 처백혀 있어. 멕이든 굶기든 내 알아서 헐 팅께."

만석은 문을 박차고 나왔다.

생각해 보면 마누라의 심정도 충분히 이해가 갔다. 뱃속에 애까지 넣고 일거리를 찾아 어딘지도 모를 곳으로 정처 없이 떠돌아야 한다는 것이 무서운 일일 것이었다. 그러나 어쩌랴. 자신은 한글도 완전히 깨치지 못한 무학(無學)에, 나이는 쉰이나 먹은 영감인 것이다. 나이를 생각하면 앞날이 캄캄해지기도 했다. 노동도 하루이틀이지 언제까지 계속할 수 있을지 의문이었다. 벌써 공사판의

requisites. After checking a few other places, his wife gave up her search.

"I'd rather go back to work at the canteen than live the life of a drifter."

"What the devil are you talking about? Are you saying you really expected we'd be staying here forever?"

At the mention of the canteen, Man-sŏk was instantly angry.

"Unplug your ears and listen well to what I'm going to say. If you don't stay put in the house where you belong, I'll break your damn legs. Whether I feed you or starve you is my business."

Kicking the door open, Man-sŏk stalked out of the house.

On second thought, though, he found her attitude about moving from place to place understandable. Facing an existence of rootless wandering must truly be frightening for a pregnant woman. Still, there was nothing to be done. Here he was, a fifty-year-old illiterate who couldn't even write the whole Hangul alphabet. The thought of his age cast a shadow across his soul. He didn't know how much longer he'd be able to go on as a manual worker. He was already being paid lower wages than the

일당도 젊은 축들과는 차이가 나게 매겨졌다.

찾아가 볼 사람이 한 사람 있긴 했다. 아파트 공사 현장 책임자인 박 기사였다. 젊은 사람이 많이 배우고 높은 자리에 있으면서도 전혀 뻐기거나 도도하지 않았다. 기술자도 아닌 막일꾼에게까지 인정스럽게 대했다. 만석은 그 박 기사와 유독 가깝게 지낸 사이였다.

만석은 몇 번을 망설인 끝에 박 기사를 찾아가기로 했다. 그에게 숨김없이 사정을 다 털어놓았다.

"딱한 사정이군요. 제가 알아볼 테니 내일 다시 만나십시다."

박 기사는 언제나처럼 정겹게 말했다.

다음 날, 박 기사는 취직자리를 만들어 놓고 기다리고 있었다.

"뭐 취직이랄 게 없군요. 아파트 관리실 소속으로 허드렛일을 해야 거든요. 월급도 너무 적고, 마음에 드실지 모르겠군요."

"고맙구만이라, 박 기사님. 지까정 것이 맘에 들고 안 들고가 워디 있간디요. 고맙구만이라."

만석은 먹구름이 가득 끼었던 가슴에 햇빛이 환히 비치는 기분으로 수없이 머리를 조아렸다.

more productive young laborers.

There was at least one person he could try to look up, an engineer named Pak, the project manager for the apartment construction he'd been working on. For a well-educated young man elevated so early to such a responsible position, he was remarkably free of arrogance. He treated even the unskilled laborers with kindness. Man-sŏk and this engineer Pak had even become rather close.

After changing his mind several times, Man-sŏk resolved to go and speak with Pak. He explained all the details of his circumstances.

"I'm sorry to hear you're in such a sad situation. Come and see me again tomorrow? I'll see what I can do," Pak said with his usual compassion.

The following day, he was waiting for Man-sŏk, a job offer in hand.

"It's not much of a position. You'll have to perform odd duties for the management office of the apartment. The pay is pretty meager, so I don't know whether you'll want to take it or not."

"Thank you very much, Mr. Pak. And let's face it, who am I to be choosy about such things. Thank you very, very much."

Man-sŏk bowed repeatedly, his clouded mind

만석은 잡역부였다. 월급은 겨우 먹고 살 정도였다. 그것만으로도 만석은 하늘의 별을 딴 기분이었다. 마누라의 소원을 풀었고, 생전 처음 월급이란 것도 타 보게 된 것이었다. 공사판 일에 비하면 아무것도 아닌 일이라서 만석은 그저 부지런히 몸을 놀렸다.

마누라는 아들을 낳았다. 왜 그렇게 기분이 좋은지 모를 일이었다. 그러나 저놈이 장가를 들려면, 생각하다가 만석은 얼굴이 굳어졌다. 스무 살에 장가를 들인다 해도 자기의 나이가 칠십이었던 것이다. 그때까지 살 수 있을까 하는 생각이 마음을 써늘하게 식혔다.

아이 하나가 더 생기자 돈이 어른 한몫이 넘게 들어갔다. 마누라는 월급이 적다고 불평을 하기 시작했다. 애가 자라나는 것에 정을 쏟으며 마누라의 투정에는 귀도 기울이지 않았다. 해가 바뀌어도 월급은 오르지 않았다. 마누라의 불평은 더 심해 갔다. 그렇다고 월급이 오를 리는 없었다. 잡역부는 임시직이었다.

산다는 것은 무엇일까. 그건 어쩌면 시나브로 세월이라는 것을 한술씩 떠 마시며 죽어 가는 것인지도 모를 일이었다. 세월을 마디마디 묶어 표시해 놓은 나이라는 것은 참 무서운 것이었다. 마흔여덟이 다르고, 마흔아홉이 다

lightened by rays of hope.

And so he became a handyman. The pay was barely enough to keep them fed, but all the same, even that paltry wage proved enough to make him feel blessed by a heavenly star. His wife's wishes could be fulfilled, and for the first time in his life he was earning a fixed salary. And because the work was light compared to what he had been used to, he made a point of being extra diligent in his duties.

His wife gave birth to a son. Why this brought him such unearthly joy he couldn't say. But at the thought that someday the little one would himself marry, Man-sŏk's face hardened. Even if the boy took a wife early, around twenty, a simple calculation told him that he would be seventy. His blood ran cold when he realized he might well die before that day came.

The addition of a child brought more new expenses than supporting a third adult possibly could have. His wife began to complain that his salary was not enough. Pouring his love into the sight of his growing child, he paid no attention to her complaints. A year went by, and there was no increase at all in the salary. His wife's complaints about

르고, 더군다나 쉰은 더 다른 얼굴이었다. 서리 내린 다음의 나뭇잎이 하루 사이로 달라지듯 늙음으로 치닫는 나이도 다급히 변색해 갔다. 한 해가 다르게 몸에서 진기가 말라 가는 것이었다.

아이놈 철수는 가난한 집 자식으로 태어날 것을 알고 미리 제 복을 타고났는지 무병하게 자랐다. 커서 부디 훌륭하게 되라고 이름도 국민학교 책에 나오는 것으로 철수라고 지었다. 날이 갈수록 생활은 쪼들려 가고 그럴수록 마누라의 찡찡거리는 소리는 심해 갔다. 그러나 만석은 아이놈에게 쏟는 정으로 이런저런 괴로움을 잊으려 했다.

아이놈이 네 살을 서너 달 앞두고였다. 관리비 절감 계획에 따라 만석은 잡역부 임시직마저 그만두지 않을 수 없게 되었다. 그건 밤길에서 만난 절벽이었다. 그렇게 앞길이 캄캄한 절망을 느낀 것은 처음이었다. 혼자 몸으로 떠돌며 끼니를 거르던 때와는 전혀 다른 절박함이고 쓰라림이었다. 당장 다음 날부터의 생계가 문제였다. 만석은 마음을 가다듬고 공사판 소식을 수소문하러 나섰다. 그래도 믿을 건 막일밖에 없었다. 며칠을 헤맨 끝에 이백 리 밖에서 벌이가 될 만한 공사가 벌어지고 있다는 걸 알아냈다.

money worsened, but they were fruitless. His handyman job was a temporary position.

What is living? Perhaps it is simply dying, slowly sipping time, spoonful by spoonful. Aging, passing the knots on the rope of time, is a fearsome thing. At forty-eight one starts to feel the slide, forty-nine is worse, and fifty has a still more oppressive face. Like the accelerating deterioration of fallen leaves after a frost, aging picks up speed as one hurtles on toward decrepitude. Your vitality dries up more and more with each passing year.

Almost as if he knew he'd been born into a poor family, Ch'ŏl-su never fell sick while growing up. Man-sŏk, hoping his child would grow to be a good man, had named him "Ch'ŏl-su" after a model boy in a grammar school reader. Still, as the days went by, life continued to become harder, and his wife's nagging grew worse and worse. Man-sŏk endeavored to forget these hardships by pouring love into his boy.

A few months before Ch'ŏl-su's fourth birthday, Man-sŏk was laid off from his job as a handyman. He was told it was due to a cutback in expenses for management of the property. He felt he was tottering on the brink of a cliff in darkness. Never before

"산 입에 거무줄 치란 법 읎다. 집 비우는 동안 철수 수발이나 잘하고 있드라고. 돈은 메칠씩 묶어 보낼 팅께."

만석은 지체하지 않고 공사판으로 떠났다.

열흘 치씩 일당을 모아 집으로 부쳤다. 쉰세 살의 몸에 남은 기운은 스스로 생각해도 믿어지지 않을 만큼 바닥이나 있었지만 만석은 이를 갈아붙였다. 그 초롱초롱한 눈을 가진 자식을 굶길 수 없다는 마음에서였다. 막일꾼에게 밥만큼 요긴한 게 술이었다. 그러나 만석은 한 홉 이상은 절대 입에 대지 않았다. 안주는 김치 깍두기로 족했다. 일당을 모아 부치는 것을 유일한 보람이요 즐거움으로 삼고 하루하루의 고달픔을 견뎌 내다 보니 두 달이 넘어가고 있었다.

그런 어느 날 만석은 편지를 받았다. 편지를 읽다 말고 만석은 벌떡 일어나며 뭐라고 소리쳤고, 비척비척하며 다시 주저앉았다.

그 길로 집에 돌아와 보니 편지에 적힌 대로 방은 썰렁하게 비어 있었고, 아무것도 모르는 아이놈은 국밥집에 맡겨져 있었다. 마누라가 젊은 놈과 도망을 가 버린 것이었다.

"개잡년, 워디 두고 보자. 내 눈에 흙 들어가기 전까지

in his life had he felt such despair. Only a man with the duties of a husband and father can understand such pain. The money would be gone by the end of the month. Man-sŏk calmed himself down and went out to try and find work; menial labor or other odd jobs were about all he could realistically seek. After several days of inquiries, he heard there was a construction project hiring about two hundred *li* away.

"No spider will ever spin its web in the mouth of this able-bodied man. While I'm gone, you just take good care of Ch'ŏl-su. I'll send money every few days."

Man-sŏk set off immediately for the work site.

He saved his wages and sent them back to his wife every ten days. There was little strength left in his fifty-three-year-old frame, but Man-sŏk gritted his teeth and worked on as hard as ever. All he could think of was that his bright-eyed little one should never go hungry, and despite the fact that alcohol is as necessary as food for a manual laborer, Man-sŏk allowed himself only a couple of small drinks a day. For supper, along with his tiny ration of liquor, he had nothing fancier than pickled cabbage or radishes. His sole pleasure in life came when he sent home the money he managed to save.

는 니년을 찾아 땅 끝까정 갈 것잉께. 잽히기만 혀 봐, 연놈 가쟁이럴 열두 갈래로 찢어 놓고 말 것잉께."

만석은 아이놈을 안아 올리며 뿌드득 이빨을 갈아붙였다. 그런 그의 눈앞에는 피바다가 된 방바닥에 내장을 다 드러내고 나자빠진 두 남녀의 시체가 역력하게 떠오르고 있었다.

"애시당초 글러묵은 기집 복이 두 번째라고 있을 턱이 읎제. 잡아 쥑이는 일만 남았응께, 워디 을매나 멀리 내빼는가 보자, 개잡년 같으니라고."

이렇게 중얼거리고 있는 만석의 입가에는 서늘한 웃음이 번지고 있었고, 눈에는 파란 살기가 서려 있었다.

사글세방의 얼마 안 되는 보증금까지 알뜰하게 챙겨 달아난 사실을 뒤늦게 알고 만석은 분에 떠밀려 주저앉고 말았다. 세간을 정리해서 몇 푼의 돈을 마련한 만석은 아이놈을 들쳐 업고 정처 없는 길을 밟았다.

누구는 서울로 갔을 거라고 했고, 어느 사람은 부산일 거라고도 했다. 다 추측에 지나지 않았다. 우선 가까운 부산부터 뒤지자고 작정하고 길을 잡았다.

때로는 굶기도 하고, 다급해지면 거렁뱅이 짓도 해 가며 도시에서 도시로 발길을 옮겼다. 젊은 나이에 일판을

In this manner two months passed.

One day a letter arrived for Man-sŏk, As he read it, he suddenly jumped to his feet, screaming. Staggering forward a few steps, he collapsed into a heap.

When he rushed directly home he found his family's room vacant and Ch'ŏl-su left in the care of one of the canteen attendants—all exactly as the letter had foretold. His wife had run away with a young man.

"Filthy bitch, you just wait! I'll chase you to the ends of the earth until my eyes are covered with dirt! As soon as I catch you, I'll tear you limb from limb!"

Man-sŏk gnashed his teeth as he lifted the child in his arms. Before his eyes floated the image of a naked man and woman floundering in a sea of blood, their guts spilling from their bodies.

"I had nothing but trouble with the first woman; why should my luck be any better with the second? All I can do now is catch her and kill her. We'll see how far you can run, you foul bitch!" he muttered to himself, a cold grin on his lips and murder in his eyes.

Discovering that Sun-im had stolen even the

따라 떠돌 때와는 달리 세상은 너무나 넓었고 또 적막했다. 비라도 추적추적 내리는 날이거나, 눈이라도 한정 없이 쏟아지는 날 같은 때는 아이놈을 품에 싸안고 만석은 소리 없는 울음을 끝없이 울었다.

한평생 산다는 것이 무언가. 나는 지금 어디로 가고 있는가. 나는 왜 이 낯선 땅에서 이러고 있는가. 사람이라는 것이 한번 잘못 태어나면 이렇게 되고 마는 것인가. 누구는 양반으로 태어나고 누구는 상것으로 태어나는가. 왜 이 세상에는 양반이고 상놈이고 하는 법이 생겨난 것일까. 다 똑같은 사람인데, 생김도 같고, 생각도 같고…… 그런데 어디서부터 그런 차등이 생긴 것일까. 내가 잘못한 것이었을까. 상놈의 피를 타고났으면 상놈답게 살아야 하는 게 순리였을까. 내 피 속에는 정말 남다른 열이 섞여 있어서 그랬을까. 서너 달 사이에 사람들을 상하게 한 죄로 이 꼴이 된 것인가…… 아니 이렇게 목숨이 붙어 있다는 것이 오히려 잘못된 것인지도 모른다. 아버지처럼 그렇게, 상것으로 취급받으며 살고 싶지는 않았다. 그것이 욕심이었을까. 상것의 턱없는 욕심이었을까. 이렇게 떠돌다가 오래지 않아 죽게 될지도 모른다. 그럼 내 새끼는 어찌되는 것인가. 이 어린것의 일생은 어찌되는 것인가. 이

deposit money for their rented room, Man-sŏk shook with redoubled rage. He gathered a paltry sum by liquidating their pitiful furnishings, picked up his son, and set off on the road with no particular destination in mind.

While some said she'd been heading for Seoul, others thought it might have been Busan. In any case, they were mere rumors. He decided to go first to Busan, simply because it was nearer.

From city to city he wandered, sometimes walking on an empty stomach, sometimes even sinking to the level of panhandling. Unlike his youthful days of drifting in search of work, the world now seemed too wide and too harsh. When it rained or snowed, the little boy whimpered quietly in Man-sŏk's arms.

What is the meaning of living? Where am I headed now? Why must I wander in this strange land? Is a common man doomed from birth? Why are some born rich and others penniless? Why has it been decreed that the world must be split into lords and slaves? People are the same, they look alike, they think alike... what can be the reason for the division? Have I been wrong to struggle? Must a born peasant be satisfied with the life of a slave? How did I become so hot-blooded? Is this state of mind a

세상 한평생을 살고 남은 건 이 새끼 하나뿐이다. 이거나마 끼고 있으니 그래도 살아갈 맘이 생기는 것인가. 내일은 또 어디로 가야 할 것인가.

만석은 괴로움을 주체할 수가 없었다.

떠돌다 보니 고향 가까이까지 이르렀다. 만석은 예나 마찬가지로 가슴이 방망이질하고 자꾸만 오금이 저려 왔다. 야음을 타고라도 한번 들러 갈까 하는 생각을 했지만 그건 순간이었다. 도저히 그럴 만한 용기가 나지 않았다.

늦은 탓일까. 전에 없이 마음이 끌리고 안타까웠다. 그동안 굳이 피했으면서도 두 번을 고향 언저리까지 접근했었다. 그때마다 밤을 이용해서였다. 그러나 서둘러 몸을 피하곤 했다. 자신의 죄는 퍼렇게 살아 있었던 것이다.

떠돌기를 일 년 반을 했을 즈음 만석은 피를 토했다. 몸이 파삭파삭 마른 것처럼 느껴졌다. 이제 머지않았다는 걸 느끼면서도 어린 자식이 마음에 걸려 행여 하는 생각과 함께 병원을 찾아갔다. 엑스레이라는 사진은 그만 살라고 말하는 모양이었다. 마누라를 찾아내는 마지막 길이라 작정하고 발길을 들여놓은 서울이었다. 그래서 이 세상을 사는 마지막 일로 생각하고 마누라와 고아원을 함께 찾으며 육 개월 동안 서울을 헤맸다. 그리고 더는 몸을 지

natural punishment for having slaughtered so many in those few months so long ago? Maybe I shouldn't have survived at all. Why couldn't I live like my father, resigned to this slave's existence? Was it greed? Was it ridiculous greed to want a better life than that of my own father? Wandering like this, I may keel over dead at any moment. What will become of my little boy then? How will he live? This child is all I have to show for my life. As long as he is with me, I still have the desire to go on living. Where am I to go tomorrow?

His agony was uncontrollable.

In his aimless wanderings Man-sŏk one day chanced upon the vicinity of his hometown. As always, his heart began to pound violently and his knees almost buckled. He considered paying a visit under the cover of night, but it was nothing more than a fleeting thought. Never would he be able to summon up the courage to return there.

Was it old age? An uncanny hunger for his lost home afflicted his troubled mind. For all those years he had avoided the place; only twice had he even come near it. Both times had been at night, and on each occasion he had fled in haste. His crime was still fresh there.

탱할 수가 없어 아들을 고아원에 맡기기로 한 것이었다. 차츰 자주 피를 토하게 된 것이다. 아이를 더 끼고 있다가는 같은 병으로 죽이게 될지도 모른다는 두려움도 컸었다.

"내 새끼덜언 요러타께 한번 키워 볼라 혔는디…… 깽가리 소리 맨치로 씨원허게 한바탕 삼시로 내 새끼덜언 쌍놈 안 맨들라고 혔는디……."

고아원을 등지고 비척비척 걸으며 영감은 중얼거리고 있었다. 꼭 실성한 것 같은 영감의 움푹 파인 볼에는 눈물이 흐르고 있었다.

영감의 흐린 시야에는 두 아들의 얼굴이 겹쳐서 어른거리고 있었다. 하나는 세 살 때 굶어 죽은 첫아들 칠봉이었고, 다른 하나는 지금 고아원에 떼 놓고 가는 두 번째 아들 철수였다.

영감은 예정했던 대로 고향으로 갈 작정이었다. 이번으로 세 번째 발길이 되는 것이다. 맞아 죽는 한이 있더라도 이번에는 고향 땅을 밟을 결심이었다.

자신이 저지른 죄로 아버지, 어머니가 분주소원에게 총살당하고 혼자 남겨진 아들 칠봉이가 굶어 죽었다는 사실을 안 것은 전쟁이 끝나서였다.

Around a year and a half after he began his wanderings in search of his wife, Man-sŏk began to spit up blood. He could feel his body wasting away with each passing day. He realized that his end was drawing near, yet clinging to a faint ray of hope for the sake of his son, he stopped at a hospital. But the X-rays only turned out to be a confirmation of his impending death. When he headed for Seoul, he knew that it would be his last chance to find Sun-im. For six months, he scoured the city for her, and then began to look for an orphanage as well, feeling that he was now completing the last mission of his life. Finally, realizing that he was unable to go on, Man-sŏk resolved to entrust his boy to an orphanage. With each day that passed, he was coughing up more blood more often. He feared that if he kept the child any longer, the fatal illness would infect him as well.

"I really meant to raise my child decently... I wanted to give him a life of true freedom, not that of a peasant's whelp..." mumbled the old man as he stumbled off, his back to the orphanage. Tears streamed down his sunken cheekbones.

Before his clouded eyes, the faces of his two sons were overlaid in one image: his first, Ch'il-bong,

"요것이 누구당가. 자네 만석이 아니라고?"

난리가 끝나고 삼 년 만에 야음을 틈타 나루터 주막에 얼굴을 내밀었을 때 황 서방은 귀신이라도 본 것처럼 놀랐다.

"자네, 워쩔라고 요러크름 왔능가? 지끔이 워쩐 세상인디?"

황 서방은 어둠으로 앞을 분간할 수 없는데도 사방을 두리번거리며 다급했다.

만석은 등을 떠밀려 방으로 들어갔다. 그러면서, 역시 못 올 곳을 왔다는 생각에 전신이 싸늘하게 굳어졌다.

"말도 마소. 자네가 내빼 뿐 바로 그날 밤으로 자네 엄니, 아부지는 총살당해 뿌렀단 마시."

"……."

만석은 굳은 돌이 되어 있었다.

"기왕 온 걸음잉께 여그서 하룻밤 보내고 낼 아침 밝기 전에 뜨소."

만약 잡히는 날에는 생매장당할 것이라고 황 서방은 괴로운 얼굴로 말했다.

"나도 나가 진 죄가 을매나 큰 것인지 알았기 땜새 그 죄 씻을라고 여그서 내뺀 그 질로 군대에 자원허지 않았

murdered at age three by the People's Army, and his second, Ch'ŏl-su, whom he'd just left behind at the orphanage.

Sticking to his plan, the old man set off for his hometown. It would be his third attempt to return. Even if he ended up stoned or beaten to death, he had made up his mind to tread once more upon the ground on which he had been born.

Only after the end of the war had he learned that his father, his mother, and his first son, Ch'il-bong, had all been executed at the hand of the People's Army.

"Who in the world is this? Aren't you Man-sŏk?"

Three years after the war, the night he had shown his face at a tavern near the ferry pier, Hwang had acted as if he'd seen a ghost.

"Why have you come back here? Don't you know how things are around here these days?"

Though it was pitch black outside, Hwang kept a nervous eye out, speaking in great haste all the while.

Soon, Man-sŏk found himself being pushed into a back room. He grew cold at the realization that he never should've returned to the place.

"It was beyond words. On the same night you ran

습디여. 삼 년 꼬빡 전쟁터를 갈고 댕김서 죽을 고비도 수십 번씩 냉김스로 뽀돗이 살아난 것인디……."

만석은 변명이라도 하듯 안타까운 표정으로 말하고 있었다.

"고거 참말이여?"

황 서방이 너무 의외라는 듯 만석의 눈을 쏘아보았다.

"황샌 앞에선 무신 상 받자고 고런 거짓말을 허겄소?"

"그랬음사 참말로 큰일 혔구만 그랴. 허나…… 고것으로 정씨 문중 사람덜 원한을 풀 수 있는 것은 아니란 말이시. 그 사람덜 원한은 시퍼렇게 남았응께. 영영 풀리기는 틀린 것일 꺼구만. 가소, 먼 디로 가서 살도록 허소."

"그래야제라. 나가 진 죄가 있는디……."

이렇게 말을 하면서도 만석은 새롭게 솟는 후회와 서러움으로 마음을 추스를 수가 없었다. 어둠에 몸을 숨겨 고향에 발을 들여놓으면서도 여기서 살게 되리라고 기대하지는 않았었다. 식구들의 안부를 알아보는 것이 목적이었다. 그런데 막상 멀리 떠나라는 말을 듣고 보니 묘한 서러움이 응어리졌다.

"지금 시상이 꼭 자네들이 깃발 들었던 그때허고 진배읎네. 달라졌다면 권이 바뀐 것이제. 참말로 험헌 시상이

away, those demons murdered your whole family. Who would've thought they were capable of slaughtering even a three-year-old?"

"..."

Man-sŏk was unable to reply; the worst of his nightmares from the past three years had suddenly become reality.

"Since you're already here you can stay with me tonight, but you must leave before sunrise tomorrow."

A pained expression on his face, Hwang said that if they caught him, he would surely be buried alive.

"I know the gravity of my crimes; that's why as soon as I got away I volunteered for service in the ROK Army. For the past three years I've fought on battlegrounds far and wide, risking death dozens of times," Man-sŏk offered, his tone apologetic.

"Really?"

Hwang was incredulous as he stared at Man-sŏk.

"What do I have to gain by lying to you'?"

"If what you've told is true, you really have done the right thing. But even so... it won't be enough to overcome the Chŏng clan's thirst for revenge. Their rage is as strong as ever. I doubt it will ever lessen. Go. Go far away and never come back!"

엎치락뒤치락이네.”

“다 지가 미친 지랄 헌 것이제라. 죄 읎는 엄니, 아부지 꺼정 잡아묵고…….”

“따지고 보면 다 자네 죄만은 아니네. 나맹키로 무식헌 것이 멀 알까마는, 시국이 죄여, 시국이. 자네헌티 죄가 있다면 성깔이 꼬치맹키로 맵고, 거그다가 쥚었다는 것이제.”

“우리 시상이 온다는 바람에…… 개돼지맹키로 산 것이 분허고 원통혀서……. 다 뜬구름 잡기였제라.”

만석은 산골짜기를 휘돌아 빠지는 거센 바람처럼 느껴지는 한숨을 길게 내쉬었다.

“난 지끔꺼정 잊어뿔지도 않네. 자네 열두 살 적이었등가? 정참봉네 재종손을 강물에 처박아 뿐 것 말이네. 그때부텀 자네 성깔은 탱자나무 까시였응께. 그 일로 자네 아부지가 을매나 고초를 당혔등가마시.”

황 서방은 안타까운 표정으로 연신 혀를 찼다.

“아부지가 나 대신 끌려가 쌔가 빠지게 당허고, 동네서 내쫓기기꺼정 혔지라우. 그때부텀 나 가슴에는 독사 대가리맹키로 원한이 맺히기 시작헌 것이제라.”

만석의 한숨 섞인 목소리가 잠겨 들었다. 자신의 생일

"You're right. I understand that my crimes can never be undone..."

As he spoke, Man-sŏk was filled with remorse. When he'd stepped once again onto the earth of his hometown, thinking himself relatively safe under the cover of darkness, he hadn't really expected to be able to live there again. All he had had in mind had been to learn what he could about his family. But now that he'd been so clearly warned to stay away, a profound sadness enveloped his heart.

"Now is no different from the day you started running. It's just that the old masters are back on top once more. The world keeps turning upside down."

"It was all because of my insanity. My blameless mother and father dead..."

"If you think over it, the blame does not fall on you alone. I may not know much, but it seems to me the times are to blame. If you committed a crime, it was because you had the fiery temper of a young man."

"It was because I wanted to believe what everybody was saying, that a new world was dawning... it enraged me that we'd been living like dogs and pigs... it was all a fit of madness."

A heavy sigh gushed forth from Man-sŏk.

날을 잊어버리는 일은 있어도 그때의 일만큼은 잊을 수가 없었다. 그러면서도 되짚어 생각하고 싶지 않은 기억이기도 했다.

강변의 갈대숲에서 서늘한 바람기가 스치는 구월이었다. 이때쯤이면 으레 짙푸르던 갈잎들이 옷갈이를 시작하는 낌새를 보이고, 털북숭이 참게는 탄탄하게 속살이 찌기 시작했다.

만석은 정참봉네 재종손 둘과 참게를 잡고 있었다. 참게는 갈밭 바위틈 같은 데 굴을 파고 살았다. 그놈들은 미련하게도 갈대꽃 줄기를 살금살금 굴속에 디밀며 놀려대면 서너 번 멈칫거리다가 그 무작스럽게 큰 집게발로 덥석 무는 것이다. 그러면 참게는 잡은 것이나 마찬가지였다. 그놈은 어찌나 미련한지 한번 집게발로 문 것은 절대로 놓는 일이 없었다. 그 집게발은 몸에서 떨어져서도 한 번 문 것은 그대로 물고 있을 지경이었다. 그래서 아이들 사이에서는, 손가락을 물리면 그대로 뎅겅 잘린다는 소문이 나 있었다. 참게를 불에 구워 간장에 찍어 먹으면 그렇게 맛이 고소한데도 아이들이 선뜻 참게를 잡으려 들지 않는 것은 손가락을 잘리게 될 무서움 때문이었다.

만석은 아이들 사이에서 참게를 잘 잡기로 이름나 있었

"I still remember it. What were you, twelve? I'm talking about the time you dunked the Chŏng family's grandson in the river. Even back then your temper had a sharp edge. Remember what a hellish time your father had because of that?"

Hwang kept tut-tutting as he spoke.

"Father was dragged away in my place, thrashed almost to death, and our family driven out of the village. That was the day the poisonous snake began growing in my heart."

Man-sŏk's voice tapered into a quiet sigh. He sometimes forgot his own birthdays, but that terrible incident—though it hadn't been anything he particularly wanted to recall—was one he'd never forgotten.

On that September day, a cool breeze caressed the bamboo groves that lined the riverbank. The green bamboo leaves were beginning to change color, and the crabs were getting fat enough to catch. Man-sŏk was gathering crabs with the Chŏng grandchildren. The little creatures hid in the crevices between the rocks in the shallow waters of the bamboo-studded shore. A stick poked slowly into the crevices was sooner or later rewarded by a dumb crab clamping onto it with its claws. That was

다. 참게 굴을 눈 빠르게 잘 찾아냈고, 참게를 신기하게도 잘 얼렀으며, 갈대꽃 줄기를 물고 늘어진 털투성이 참게를 용케도 잘 다루는 것이었다. 만석의 이런 솜씨를 보며 아이들은 그저 감탄하고 부러워했다.

만석이 이렇게 되기까지에는 아이들이 모르는 고통을 혼자 겪어 냈던 것이다. 만석이 강변을 따라 질펀하게 펼쳐진 갈대숲을 뒤지기 시작한 것은 여섯 살 때부터였다. 갈숲에는 남모르게 배를 채울 것이 심심찮게 있었던 것이다. 봄에는 물새알, 여름에는 물새 새끼, 가을에는 참게, 만석은 그런 것들로 허기진 배를 채웠다. 꽁보리밥도 제대로 먹지 못하는 속은 언제나 헛헛하고 쓰렸다. 배를 채우기 위해서는 참게의 집게발 따위는 그렇게 무서울 게 없었다. 처음 얼마 동안은 안 물린 손가락이 없었다. 일단 손가락을 물리면 재빨리 참게를 땅바닥에 패대기를 쳐야 한다. 그러면 집게발이 몸에서 떨어지고, 그다음 아픔을 참아 내며 살을 파고드는 집게발을 떼 내야 하는 것이다. 그런데 참게 몸뚱어리를 집게발에서 떼 내지 않은 채 손가락을 빼내려고 덤비면 또 하나 남아 있던 집게발에 다른 손을 물리기 십상이었다. 두 집게발에 양쪽 손의 손가락을 하나씩 물리는 신세가 되면 어찌될 것인가.

all there was to actually catching them. They were so stupid that once they grabbed onto anything, they never let go; even when their claws were cut from their body they remained tightly clamped. It was easy to see why the kids always said that a finger pinched in those claws would end up having to be cut off. And so while roast crab dipped in soy sauce was incredibly tasty, the children were so afraid of losing their fingers that they were often reluctant to do much crab-catching.

Among these same children, however, Man-sŏk was renowned as a first-rate crab catcher. And it was true: he was quick to discover the holes where they hid, unusually good at luring them out, and quite skillful at dealing with them once they'd latched onto a bamboo stick. Witnessing his prowess, the other children were in awe.

Unbeknownst to his little peers, Man-sŏk had endured much suffering in solitude in order to amass these formidable skills. From the age of six, he had frequently foraged for food in the bamboo groves along the river. He had always been able to find something there to fill his empty stomach. Waterbird eggs in springtime, hatchling birds in summer, and crabs in the autumn had been the

거의 안 물린 손가락이 없을 정도로 혼자 고통을 당하는 사이에 만석은 능숙한 솜씨로 참게를 다룰 수 있게 된 것이었다. 참게한테 물릴 때의 아픔은 대단한 것이었다. 눈에서 불꽃이 번쩍하는 것 같기도 하고, 자지 끝이 맵게 쏘이는 것 같기도 했다. 그러고는 손가락이 빠져나가는 것처럼 아파지는 것이다. 그러나 손가락이 잘려 나가지는 않았다. 눈앞이 노래지며 무릎이 자꾸 꺾이는 배고픔을 없앨 수 있다면 그까짓 아픔쯤 아무것도 아니었던 것이다.

그런데 다른 애들은 그 아픔이 무서워 참게를 잡을 엄두를 못 냈고, 특히 정씨네 문중 아이들은 참게가 털투성이의 다리 열 개를 마구 내두르는 모습만 보고도 뒷걸음질을 쳤다. 만석은 그런 그들을 마음속으로 비웃고 무시했다. '느그덜이 양반 부잣집 자석들이라 내가 지는 것이여. 그런 것 싹 읎애 뿔고 혀본다면 다 한주먹 밥잉께.' 이런 속말을 하고 있었다.

그날 정참봉네 재종손이 고구마 세 개를 내밀며 참게 다섯 마리를 잡아 달라고 했던 것이다. 별로 밑지는 장사는 아니어서 만석은 그러기로 했다. 잘 삶아진 밤고구마를 우물거리며 만석은 참게 잡기에 열중했다. 네 마리째를 잡느라고 갈대꽃 줄기를 까딱까딱 놀리고 있는데 느닷

resources best able to ease his pangs of hunger. The bowls of barley he got at home never even come close to killing his hunger, and his belly had always seemed empty. Compared to his need for food, his fear of the pinching claws of the crabs was nothing. When he first began, not a single one of his fingers was free from claw cuts. He soon learned that when a crab pinched a finger, he had to quickly dash it on a rock with all his might, which would rip the claw from the crab's body. Then he could pry it loose: a painful process. If he tried to take the whole crab off, the free claw was likely to lock onto one of his other fingers. If the two claws were to grab a finger on each hand, there would be no escape.

Through this pain-filled period of solitary trial and error, Man-sŏk was gradually able to teach himself to deal skillfully with the little crabs. The pain of being pinched by their claws was indescribable. At first it felt as if his eyes were on fire or the tip of his penis had been stung. Then it felt like his fingers were being ripped off—though no fingers were ever actually lost. Still, such pain was nothing, Man-sŏk had decided, as long as it allowed him to eat, to diminish that gnawing hunger that yellowed his

없는 비명소리가 울렸다. 만석은 벌떡 몸을 일으켰다.

참게를 담은 조그만 항아리 옆에 쪼그리고 앉았던 정참봉네 재종손 둘 중에 동생이 숨이 넘어가고 있었다. 아홉 살 먹은 그놈은 자지러지게 비명을 지르며 팔딱팔딱 뛰고 있었는데, 허공을 내젓고 있는 팔, 그 손가락에는 참게가 매달려 있었다. 그리고 만석이와 동갑인 그의 형은 "엄니, 엄니" 외치며 어쩔 줄을 모르고 있었다. 보나마나 항아리를 기어오르려고 버둥대는 참게를 보며 장난질을 치다가 손가락을 덥석 물린 것이었다.

만석은 재빨리 달려가서 날뛰고 있는 녀석의 팔을 붙들고는 아래로 힘껏 뿌렸다. 그래도 참게는 손가락에 매달려 있었다. 손바닥을 땅에 대게 했다. 그리고 뒤꿈치로 참게를 짓밟았다. 몸통이 으깨지며 집게발이 떨어졌다. 언제나 마찬가지로 집게발은 그대로 손가락을 물고 있었다. 녀석은 계속 숨넘어가는 비명을 지르고 있었고, 만석은 빠른 솜씨로 집게발을 벌려 손가락에서 떼 냈다. 그때였다.

"요런 개자석!"

이런 욕과 함께 만석의 눈에서 불이 번쩍했다. 참게에 물린 녀석의 형이 주먹으로 만석의 볼을 갈긴 것이다.

"워째 이려?"

vision and weakened his knees.

The other children didn't dare to catch crabs for fear of that very pain. Especially the Chŏng kids, who ran off in a fright at the mere sight of a crab brandishing its claws. Man-sŏk looked down on these cowards and sneered, thinking to himself, "I have to let them get the best of me only because they are Chŏngs. If it wasn't for that, I could knock them out with one blow."

The following day, one of the Chŏng grandsons offered him three sweet potatoes if Man-sŏk would catch five crabs for him. Finding the bargain acceptable, Man-sŏk agreed to do it. His mouth full of well-cooked sweet potato, he was soon absorbed in his crab hunting. As he twirled his bamboo stick in search of the fourth crab, he suddenly heard a scream. Man-sŏk instantly jumped to his feet.

The younger of the two Chŏng grandsons, the one who'd been squatting near the small pot where the captured crabs were kept, looked like he was drawing his last breath. The nine year-old boy was shrieking his lungs out and hopping about like a fish out of water, his arms whirling through the air. A crab dangled from one of his fingers. His older brother, who was Man-sŏk's age, didn't know what

너무 느닷없는 일이라서 만석은 어리둥절해서 물었다.

"몰라서 물어?"

다시 주먹이 날아왔다. 피할 겨를도 없이 맞으며 만석은 자기가 잘못을 뒤집어쓰고 있다는 것을 직감했다. 만석은 기막힌 기분이 되면서 서너 발짝 뒤로 물러섰다.

"니 심뽀 나가 다 앙께로 더 지랄허지 말어."

만석은 맞서 싸울 태세를 갖추며 소리쳤다. 그런 만석의 입은 앙다물어졌고, 눈빛은 험악하게 변해 있었다. 그런 기세에 놀랐는지 큰녀석이 주춤했다.

"우리 동상이 물린 것은 니 땜새 그런 것잉께, 존 말로 헐 찌게 니 두 손 다 저그다 쑤셔 박어!"

큰녀석이 참게가 든 항아리를 가리켰고, 작은녀석은 손가락을 들여다보며 서럽게 울고 있었다.

"멋이여?"

만석은 속이 뒤집히는 걸 느꼈다. 또 상것이기 때문에 당해야 하는 억울함에 부딪히고 있는 것이었다. 그 억울함은 말로 되느 것이 아니었다. 억지였기 때문에 언제나 말이 필요 없었다. 말은 아무 소용이 없었다. 시키는 대로 하는 것만 남아 있었다.

그러나 지금 참게가 든 항아리 속에 손을 넣을 수는 없

to do except to shout "Mommy! Mommy!" Undoubtedly, the little one had been pinched as he played with the crabs that were trying to escape from the jar.

Man-sŏk ran over to the boy, grabbed his arm and dashed the crab to the ground as hard as he could. Even then, the crab was still clinging to the boy's finger. Man-sŏk had him lay his hand on the ground. Then with his heel, Man-sŏk crushed the crab. The mashed body tore away from the claw, which, as always, stayed embedded in the finger. The boy was still wailing louder than ever when Man-sŏk quickly and deftly pried the claw off his finger. At that very moment, he heard the voice:

"You little bastard!"

No sooner had he heard it than he was seeing stars. The elder Chŏng brother had punched Man-sŏk square in the face with his fist.

"What was that for?"

The blow had come out of nowhere, and Man-sŏk's first reaction was to be puzzled.

"You know very well why!"

Another blow landed. Though he'd lacked time to dodge the second blow, Man-sŏk suddenly realized he was being set up to take the blame. Dumbfounded, he retreated several steps.

었다. 잘못이 있고 없고가 문제가 아니었다. 저놈은 어른도 아니고 자기와 동갑인 것이다. 그런 놈이 시키는 대로 할 수는 없었다. 그러느니 차라리 칵 죽어 버리는 것이 나을 것이었다.

"아, 얼렁 못 넣겄어!"

큰녀석이 소리쳤고,

"죽었으면 죽었제 고러케는 못허겄구만!"

만석은 입가에 비웃음을 물며 맞섰다.

"워쩌? 니까징 것이 대들어? 참말로 죽어야 니가 맛을 알겄다 그것이제. 야, 동진아, 저놈 새끼럴 오늘 반쯤 쥑여 뿔자!"

큰녀석이 동생에게 말했고, 둘이는 주먹을 말아 쥐고 다가들었다.

"이눔아, 존 일 헌다고 말썽 피우지 마라. 사람은 지 태생을 알아야 쓰는 법이여. 그저 죽어지내는 기 상수여."

크고 작은 말썽이 일어날 때마다 순하디 순한 아버지는 이렇게 되풀이하곤 했다. 두 녀석이 합세해서 달려들고 있는 다급함 속에서도 아버지의 그 말이 번뜩 떠올랐다. 그러나 이대로 몰매를 맞을 수는 없었다.

만석은 획 날아드는 주먹을 피했다. 아무리 못 먹고 살

"I see what you're trying to do, so just cut it out!" shouted Man-sŏk, preparing to defend himself. His jaw was set, and his eyes gleamed ferociously. The Chŏng boy was shocked by this display and grew hesitant.

"It was your fault that my brother got bitten! So you'd better do what I say and put both your hands in there!"

The older boy pointed at the pot full of crabs. The little one was still crying and examining his finger.

"What?"

Man-sŏk's stomach tied itself into a knot. He knew that it was only because he was a lowly peasant child that he faced this injustice. The demand was utterly senseless, but words would be of no use. All that was left for him to do was follow the orders, but even as this thought occurred to him he realized that he was simply incapable of putting his own hands into the jar full of crabs. Whether or not he was actually at fault was no longer the point. He wasn't even being confronted by an adult; it was only a boy his own age. Why should he have to obey him? Man-sŏk decided that he would rather die than do what the boy demanded.

"Go on, right now!" the boy shouted.

긴 했지만 열 살이 못 되어 나뭇짐을 지기 시작했고, 열 살이 넘으면서부터는 지게질을 한 몸이었다. 싸움하는 기술만큼은 기름지게 먹고 큰 정씨네 문중의 아이들 둘쯤은 식은 죽 먹기였다

만석은 한 방으로 싸움에 이기는 법을 알고 있었다. 헛손질을 한 큰녀석이 숨을 씩씩대며 다시 달려들고 있었다. 만석은 녀석의 사타구니를 겨냥해서 그대로 발을 날렸다. 달려들던 녀석은 소리도 제대로 못 지르며 나가떨어져 버르적거렸다. 불알을 차인 것이었다.

"성, 성, 일어나, 일어나랑께!"

작은녀석이 파랗게 질려 뒹굴고 있는 제 형을 흔들어대고 있었다.

"니놈도 내 주먹 맛 잠 봐야 써!"

만석은 작은녀석의 멱살을 잡아 일으켜 사정없이 후려갈겼다. 만석은 이미 제정신이 아니었다. 성질이 칼칼하고 불같은 그는 한번 홍분하면 걷잡지를 못했다. 그래서 그의 어머니는 '지리산 호랭이가 칵 씹어 갈 성깔머리'라고 욕하곤 했다.

만석은, 이놈들을 아무도 모르게 죽여 버려야 되겠다는 무서운 생각을 하고 있었다. 더 두들겨 패서 강물에 처박

"I'd rather drop dead!"

Man-sŏk sneered as he answered.

"What?! A thing like you dares to talk back to me?! You really want to die? Hey, Dong-jin, let's kill this bastard!"

The elder Chŏng boy called to his younger brother, and both of them approached with clenched fists.

"My dear boy, don't make trouble, if things don't always go your way. A man ought to know his place. It's best to just go on and do as ordered."

Such had been the words of his good-hearted father whenever trouble arose. Now, at this moment of truth, when these two boys joined together to attack him, he recalled his father's words of admonition. But he was unable to simply stand and expose himself to their blows.

Man-sŏk parried the first punch. Though he had grown up hungry, he had also grown up working, carrying firewood before he turned ten, and, after that, working as a porter for shouldering heavy loads; he was strong. When it came to fighting skills, the two well-fed Chŏng children were no match for him at all.

Man-sŏk knew the secret of winning a fight with a

아 버리자는 생각이 머리를 스쳤다. 그래서 두 녀석을 정신을 잃을 때까지 팼고, 하나씩 질질 끌어 강가로 옮기다가 동네 어른들에게 들킨 것이었다.

아버지는 정씨 문중에 끌려가 반죽음이 되도록 얻어맞고 업혀 왔고, 겨우 기동을 하게 되었을 때 내쫓기는 신세가 되었다. 아버지는 한 번만 살려 달라고 땅에 엎드려 울며 빌었고, 정씨 문중 사람들은 달구지에 세간살이를 실어 내서 강가에다 부려 버렸다. 아버지는 강 건너 산비탈에다 움막을 지어야 했고, 정씨 문중의 소작을 잃어버린 생활은 굶는 것이 곧 먹는 것이 되고 말았다. 그러나 아버지는 만석을 때리거나 나무라지 않았다.

"니는 천상 느그 할아부지럴 빼박은 것이여. 쌍놈으로 살기는 피가 너무 뜨건 것이제."

몸을 가누지 못하고 앓아누운 아버지는 혼잣말처럼 중얼거리며 주르륵 눈물을 흘렸던 것이다.

아버지가 정씨 문중의 용서를 받고 다시 옛집으로 이사를 한 것은 사 년이 지나서였다.

"행여 아부지, 엄니 산소는 원처케……."

만석은 망설이고 망설였던 말을 힘겹게 하고는 고개를 떨구었다.

single blow. The older Chŏng boy, whose first punch failed to land, lunged again, breathlessly. Man-sŏk aimed a kick at his crotch. The boy couldn't even scream as he flew onto his back and lay there, squirming. His balls had been hit.

"Brother! Brother! Get up! Get up, I say!"

The younger Chŏng boy was shaking his brother as he writhed on the ground, his face white.

"You two deserve a taste of my fist."

Man-sŏk pulled the little one up by the collar and began mercilessly showering him with blows. He was no longer in his right mind. Once his hot temper took over, there was no controlling it. His mother often said that only a mountain tiger from Jirisan could get the better of that temper.

It occurred to Man-sŏk that he could kill the two boys without anybody ever knowing that he had done it. The thought flashed into his mind that he ought to thrash them some more and then throw them into the river. And so he beat them senseless. As he dragged one of them to the riverside, however, one of the grown-ups in the village caught sight of him.

His father was brought before the Chŏng family, and it wasn't until they had beaten him half to death

"자네 볼 면목이 읎네. 살기등등헌 그 등살에 누가 묘 쓰겄다고 나섰겄는가, 무담씨 화 당헐까 벼 나부텀 꽁지를 사린 인심 아니었등가."

황 서방이 솔직하게 말했고, 만석은 고개를 떨군 채 아무 반응도 없었다.

만석이 이 말을 입에 올렸던 것은 혹시라도 부모님 묘가 있으리라는 기대감을 가져서가 아니었다. 마지막으로 마음을 거두는 땅인데, 그 사실을 확인하고 싶었던 것이다.

반동치고 그보다 더한 반동이 있었을까. 그 누가 감히 시체를 거둬 주려 나섰을 것인가. 어느 구덩이에 한꺼번에 묻히고 말았을 것이다.

"황샌, 고맙구만이라. 인자 가 봐야 쓰겄소."

만석은 일어섰다.

"아니, 무신 소리여. 눈 한숨 붙이고 닭 울기 전에 떠나랑께."

"아니어라우. 고연시리 새복에 움직기리다가 넘덜 눈에 띄면 황샌 입장만 바늘방석잉께요. 지금이 숨어 가기는 질 좋겄구만이라."

"요러케 가뿔 줄 알았으면 주먹밥이라도 얼렁 한 덩이 맨들었을 것인디."

that he was carried back home on somebody's back. When his father recovered enough to be able to walk, their family was expelled from the village. His father had groveled on the ground, weeping as he begged for mercy, but the Chŏngs had refused to hear any of it. Instead, the men of the Chŏng family loaded all of Man-sŏk's family's household goods onto a cart and dumped it near the river. Man-sŏk and his father had nothing left to do but to build a makeshift shack on the far side. As they were no longer able to sharecrop the Chŏng land, they found their lifeline completely severed; there was no food to had. And yet, even then, Man-sŏk's father never laid a hand on him or reproached him.

"You are the spitting image of your grandfather: too hot-blooded to lead the bound life of a peasant," he muttered from his sickbed, tears streaming down his face.

It had been four years before his father was finally forgiven by the Chŏngs and allowed to return to the house in the village.

"What about the graves of my parents...?" Man-sŏk asked, dropping his head and overcoming his hesitation.

"황샌, 그때 나 살려 준 은혜 평생 잊지 않을 것이구만이라."

"아니여, 아니여. 자네나 나나 다 피 잘못 받고 태어난 죄밖에 읎는 목심들이여. 자네 속 내 다 알어. 실로 따지고 보면 나 같은 남자가 보잘것읎는 쫌팽이여. 한목심 편차고 이래도 웃고, 저래도 웃고 사는 나 같은 것은 속창아리도 읎는 빙신잉께. 나 같은 것에 비길라 치면 자네는 을매나 남자다운가. 정작 남자는 자넨 것이여. 그렁께 나헌테 은혜 입었다는 소리는 날 욕허는 소리여. 자네 숨은 디를 안 갤차 준 것은 자네맹키로 힘지게 못산 나 같은 짜잔헌 사내가 마땅히 혀야 헐 일이었응께."

황 서방의 눈에는 물기가 어리고 있었다.

"황샌, 오래오래 사시씨요."

만석은 목이 메어 깊이 고개를 숙였다.

"다 잊어뿔고, 다 잊어뿔고, 크게 한바탕 살아 보소. 그것이 이기는 질잉께."

만석은 어둠 속에서 황 서방과 헤어졌다.

어둠 속에서 눈이 차츰 익자 강줄기가 희뿌옇게 드러났다. 그 강줄기를 바라보며 만석은 움직일 줄을 몰랐다. 나룻배로 강을 건너면 고향 마을이었다.

"It pains me to tell you this, but everybody was so scared of the murderers that no one dared to claim the bodies."

Hwang spoke honestly, but Man-sŏk just hung his head and didn't reply. Man-sŏk, in inquiring, hadn't really expected that his parents would have been given a decent burial. He just wanted to confirm his fears, as he was realizing that he would never again be returning to this land.

There could have been no worse reactionary than he himself in the eyes of the villagers at that time. His parents and three-year-old son must have faced a death more cruel than that meted out to anyone else. Who indeed would have courage enough to claim the corpses? They were probably dumped together into a hole.

"Thank you, indeed. I must be on my way now."

Man-sŏk got up.

"Why, what are you talking about? Sleep a while and you can leave before the cock crows."

"No, really, if I happen to be seen, it'll surely put you in an awkward position. No better time than now to sneak out."

"Had I known you'd be going so soon, I would've made you some food for the journey."

등 뒤에서 총소리가 콩볶듯 하기 시작한 것은 만석이 서낭당을 지났을 무렵이었다. 총소리 사이사이로 왁자한 사람들의 외침이 들리기도 했다. 불이 붙도록 다급한 마음과는 달리 만석은 빨리 뛸 수가 없었다. 하루 종일 왕복 백 리 길을 걸은 다음이라 지칠 만큼 지쳐 있었던 것이다. 총소리는 차츰 가깝게 들리고 있었다. 만석이 강변 나루터에 도착했을 때 황 서방은 배를 대 놓고 있던 참이었다.

"화, 황샌, 나 잠 살려 주씨요."

"자네, 워쩐 일여?"

"분주소장을 쥑여 뿌렀소. 얼렁 배를 잠 띄우씨요."

"자네 미쳤능가? 배 띄웠다가는 둘 다 강 복판에서 죽게 되야. 싸게 갈밭으로 내빼, 갈밭으로. 지끔 안개가 피기 시작혔고, 금방 어두워질 것잉께. 아, 싸게 내빼란 마시."

황 서방은 발을 굴렀다. 만석은 갈대밭으로 뛰어들었다.

소쩍새 울음빛 같은 노을이 강물을 태우고 있었고 강변으로는 서서히 저녁 물안개가 피어오르고 있었다. 갈대밭에는 애기 울음 같은 소리를 내며 바람이 지나가고 있었고, 갈숲은 바람 타는 물결처럼 쇠아쇠아 흔들리고 있었다. 만석은 안심하고 있는 힘을 다해 갈밭을 기고 있었다. 이 정도로 갈숲이 바람을 타면 사람 하나쯤이 흔들어 내

"I will never forget that you saved my life."

"No, no. You and I, our only crime was to be born into a low bloodline. I understand perfectly well how you feel. If you think on it, I'm the one that's worthless. A spineless fool who smiles at this and that just for the sake of an easy existence. Compared to a thing like me, you've been a courageous man. You've been a real man. For you to speak of your indebtedness to me is an insult. Not revealing your hiding place was only natural; it was the least a nobody like me could do for you."

Tears were welling up in Hwang's eyes.

"Live a long life," Man-sŏk said in a faltering voice.

"Forget everything, forget it all, and enjoy your life for a change. That's the way for you to win."

Man-sŏk bid farewell to Hwang in darkness.

As his eyes gradually adjusted to the night, the river came into focus as if a mist was clearing. He stood very still, watching the flowing water. Just across the river by the ferry lay the hamlet where he had been born.

It was as Man-sŏk ran past the village shrine that bursts of machine gun fire began sounding behind him. Interspersed with the shots were yells and

는 것도 표도 안 나는 것이었다. 어렸을 때부터 갈대밭에 드나들어 체득했던 것이다.

강변에서 서너 발의 총성이 울린 것은 만석이 질펀한 갈대밭 중간쯤에 이르렀을 때였다. 만석은 어둠이 짙어지기를 기다렸다가 강물로 뛰어들었다. 큰길을 피해서 산을 탔다.

그때 자신의 목숨은 황 서방의 손가락 끝에 매달려 있었던 것이다.

칠월 초순에서부터 구월 초순까지, 만석 자신이 누린 그 꿈만 같던 세월은 고작해야 두 달이었다. 그동안 만석은 정말이지 세상이 다 자기 것인 줄 알았었다.

노동자, 농민을 해방시킨다고 했다. 부자나 지주들을 쳐 없애고 상것들이 모든 행세를 하는 것이라 했다. 만석은 생각하고 자시고 할 필요가 없었다. 그는 물 만난 고기였다.

만석이 제일 먼저 해치운 일이 정씨 문중의 사당을 불지른 것이었다. 불길에 휩싸이는 사당을 바라보며 만석은 소리치고 있었다.

"지금부텀 정씨놈덜 씨를 말려 뿔 것이여. 좆 달린 것이라면 한 마리도 안 냉기고 싹 쓸어 뿔 것이라고."

shouts. Though his mind was racing, he wasn't able to run very fast at all; having already trudged a hundred *li* that day, he was about to drop from exhaustion. The guns were getting closer with each passing second. When he reached the ferry, Hwang was about to cast off the boat's line for a crossing.

"Hwang! Please help me!"

"What's wrong?"

"I killed the People's Army commander! Hurry and let's shove off!"

"Are you crazy? If we cross now, both of us will be sitting ducks in the middle of the river! Hurry and hide in the bamboo grove! Get to the bamboo! The fog is settling in, and it'll be dark soon. What are you waiting for? Go right now and hide!"

Hwang was impatient, almost straining to run himself.

Man-sŏk dashed into the stand of bamboo.

The water burned in the sunset, its color as uncanny as the screech of an owl, and fog gradually enveloped the riverbanks. The wind sounded like a crying child as it whipped through the bamboo, rolling in waves over the leaves. Feeling safer now, Man-sŏk burrowed deeper into the grove. The blustery wind was noisy enough to smother any sounds

시퍼런 낫을 휘두르며 소리치는 만석의 앞에 그 누구도 얼씬거리지 못했다. 만약 누가 대들었다면 휘둘러대는 낫에 뎅겅 목이 달아나고 말았을 것이다.

발이 빠른 사람들은 더러 피신을 하기도 했지만 그렇지 못한 정씨 문중 남자들은 다 잡혀서 끌려갔다. 그리고 반 죽음이 되도록 두들겨 맞고는 날마다 한 사람씩 뒷등 소나무에 묶여서 죽어 갔다.

최씨네 사람들은 어느 집이나 밥을 굶었다. 곡식이란 곡식을 모조리 빼앗겼기 때문에 죽도 끓일 것이 없었다.

"안 되야, 안 되야. 즘생도 고러크름 야박허게 다루는 것이 아닌디, 워째 사람을 그랄 수가 있드라냐. 어린 새끼덜이 있는디 죽이라도 쑤게는 혀야 혀. 만석아, 이눔아, 맴 돌려서낭은 죽이라도 끓이게 맹길어. 애비 쥑인 웬수라도 고러케 허는 벱이 아닌 것이여."

아버지는 만석에게 매달리며 애원했다.

"아부지는 평생 당허고만 산 일이 치가 떨리지도 안 혀서 그런다요?"

만석은 아버지를 뿌리치며 눈을 치떴다.

"고런 못된 소갈머리 버려야 써. 미우나 고우나 그 사람덜이 우리럴 믹여살린 것이여."

he made while crawling about. It was a familiar place; he had foraged the riverside bamboo since he had been old enough to walk.

Just as he got to the center of the grove, he heard several shots go off on the riverbank. Man-sŏk waited for the night to thicken before jumping into the river. Staying clear of the main paths, he made his way up the mountain.

His life had hung by a thread from the tips of Hwang's fingers.

Man-sŏk's dreamlike world of power had only lasted from July until early September: two brief months. During that time, however, he had actually felt that the entire world was his to command.

They had said that the peasants and workers would be liberated. They had told him, too, that the landlords and the rich would be liquidated and all the power seized by the exploited. There'd been no need for Man-sŏk to think twice about it. He had taken to the new order like a fish to water. He had taken up his sickle, freshly honed on the whetstone, and murder had lit up his eyes.

Man-sŏk's first settling of accounts was to set the Chŏngs ancestral shrine ablaze. Watching the tower of flames, he cried out:

"아부지, 참말로 고런 말만 골라서 허실라요? 아부지, 고런 맘일랑 안 고쳐묵으면 워치께 되는지 아시겄소? 정가놈덜허고 똑같은 꼴 당헌단 말이요."

만석은 싸늘한 표정으로 말했고.

"하먼이라. 아부님 말씸은 쪼깨 과헌 성싶구만이라. 원제 그 사람덜이 우리 믹여살렸습디여. 우리가 쌔 빠지게 일혀서 고것들 팅팅 살찌게 혔고, 우리사 쭉징이만 묵고 포돗이포돗이 살았제라."

며느리가 눈을 희게 뜨며 남편을 거들고 나섰다.

천 씨는 그만 입을 다물고 말았다. 며느리까지 생판 딴 사람으로 변한 지가 오래였다. 사람이 맘이 변하면 죽는 일을 당한다고 했다. 아들도 며느리도 제정신이 아닌 것이다. 아들놈은 사람 백정 노릇을 눈 하나 깜짝 안 하고 해내고 있고, 며느리는 그 얌전하던 옛 모습을 하루아침에 벗어 버리고 꼭 화냥년처럼 변했다. 아들놈하고 똑같이 며느리도 여맹 부위원장이 되어 날쳐대고 있는 것이다. 그 예쁜 얼굴에 눈 한번 제대로 뜨지 않던 며느리가 그렇게 변한 것이 못내 서운했다. 아니, 사람을 그렇게 돌변시켜 버리는 그 공산당이란 것이 생각할수록 겁나고 무서워졌다.

"From this day on, I won't rest till I wipe out all the seed of the Chŏng clan! Not a single Chŏng with a dangling cock will be left alive!"

He brandished the razor-sharp sickle as he shouted, and not a soul dared approach him. Anybody trying to stop him would have had his throat cut in the wink of an eye.

A few of the quicker ones managed to escape, but most of the men in the Chŏng family were seized and taken away. They were beaten half to death and then killed, one by one; each day another was bound to the pine tree on the hillside and executed.

Though each day witnessed another such death, no funeral biers departed the Chŏng house, for the family was unable to claim the bodies. Everyone in the Chŏng household went hungry. They were robbed of all their stores, down to their last grain of rice.

Man-sŏk's father grabbed him and begged him to relent.

"No, it's wrong, I tell you. It's wrong. You wouldn't treat beasts with such cruelty. How can you treat human beings this way? They have little children, and not even the makings for gruel have been left to them. Man-sŏk, think again and at least allow

만석은 날개를 있는 대로 편 독수리가 되어 제멋대로 날아다니느라고 제 발밑에서 불이 붙고 있는 것은 까맣게 모르고 있었다. 마누라가 말 한마디로 모든 것을 척척 해내는 분주소장에게 정신이 팔려 있다는 사실을 낌새도 채지 못했다. 피곤하다는 이유로 잠자리의 요구를 물리치곤 했을 때도 의심은커녕 혁명 과업을 완수하느라고 낮에 고생한 아내를 괴롭히는 것 같아 오히려 미안하게 생각했던 것이다.

만석은 인민의용군에 붙들려 가지 않으려고 벽촌으로만 피해 다녔다. 그러면서 밤마다 그 험악한 꿈에 시달렸다. 두 연놈이 알몸뚱이로 뒹굴고 있었고, 피바다가 된 방바닥에 배창자가 터져 나온 두 연놈이 나자빠져 있는 광경이었다.

밥을 먹다가 언뜻 그 생각이 떠오르면 구역질이 치밀어 더는 먹을 수가 없었다. 한 달 가까이 피해 다니다가 인민군이 싸움에 져서 거의가 산속으로 도망을 치고 있다는 소식을 들었다. 그런 사고가 없이 그대로 고향에 있었더라면 자신은 어떻게 됐을까를 만석은 곰곰이 생각해 보았다. 세상은 다시 뒤바뀐 것이다. 틀림없이 몸을 피한 정씨 문중 사람들이 들이닥칠 것이었다. 인민군을 따라 도망칠

them some food. Even if they'd murdered your kin, treating them like this wouldn't be right."

"Enough reactionary foolishness! You've been walked on your whole life! Doesn't it make you shudder just to think of it?"

Man-sŏk glared and shrugged off his father's grasp.

"To look at it that way is a mistake. Whether you like them or hate them, they have kept food in our mouths."

"Father, are you really going to talk like that? If you don't wake up, do you know what'll happen to you? The same thing that happened to the Chŏngs will happen to you!"

Man-sŏk went on, his tone icy:

"It's true. And you, Father, go too far. When did they ever feed us? We were always the ones who broke our backs to keep them fat, and all we got was the chaff to keep us scrawny."

The daughter-in-law excitedly concurred with her husband's upbraiding of his father.

Man-sŏk's father had no choice but to shut his mouth. His daughter-in-law had undergone a complete transformation of late. It is said that such a total change in personality is a sign of approaching

수밖에 다른 도리가 없었을 것 같았다.

이제 전쟁은 다 끝났다. 그러나 뒷정리까지 다 끝난 것은 아니었다. 타작을 끝내고 나면 청소를 할 뒷일이 남는 거나 마찬가지였다. 산으로 도망갔던 공비가 밤이면 여기저기 출몰했고, 전에 부역했던 사람들이 색출되고 있는 참이었다.

"보나마나 뻔한 일 아니겄능가. 더러 산사람이 되기도 혔고, 눈치 못 채고 뒤처진 축들은 잽혀서 또 그 징헌 꼴 안 당했드랑가."

황 서방은 더 길게 얘기하고 싶지 않다는 듯 고개를 설레설레 저었다.

만석은 강줄기처럼 긴 한숨을 내쉬었다. 그리고 천천히 어둠 속을 걸었다. 황 서방의 말대로 멀리 떠나서 사는 길밖에 없었다. 이제 얻은 것도, 남은 것도 아무것도 없는 것이다. 허망하기도 했고 어이가 없기도 했다.

그렇게 학교라는 것이 다녀 보고 싶었다. 그러나 아무나 배우는 것이 아니라고 했다. 상것은 상것대로 할 일이 따로 있다고 했다. 그것이 나무하는 일이었고, 지게질이었고, 소 꼴 뜯기는 일이었다. 정씨네 아이들이 나무 그늘에서 수박이나 참외를 배 터지게 먹으며 히히덕거리고 있

death. To him, neither his son nor his son's wife seemed to be in their right minds. His beloved son was now a butcher who could commit murder without blinking, and his daughter-in-law, once a prim and proper woman, had begun to act like a slut overnight. Like Man-sŏk, she had taken to the new order, becoming a Vice-Chairman of the Women's Brigade of the People's Militia, and she, too, was soon in a frenzy. It saddened him indeed to witness the unbelievable change in his shy and pretty daughter-in-law. The more he thought about how this thing called "the Communist Party" was able to change a person overnight, the more horrified he became.

Man-sŏk, like a bird of prey gliding on outstretched wings, was too busy flying over his territory to notice the fire burning right under his feet. He hadn't had the slightest notion that his wife was crazy about the People's Army commander, who always wore a gun and determined who would live and who would die with a single word. When she had rejected Man-sŏk's advances in bed, saying she was too tired, not only had he not grown suspicious, he had actually felt sorry to have bothered her when she had been working so hard for the

을 때 자기는 땡볕 속의 논길을 이리 뛰고 저리 뛰며 새를 쫓느라 목이 터지게 소리를 질러야 했다. 겨울이면 으레 아이들의 책보를 모아들고 학교까지 가야 했다. 그 아이들은 자기보다 몇 배 두꺼운 솜옷에 장갑까지 끼고는 손이 시려서 책보를 못 들고 간다는 것이었다.

인절미 두 개를 얻어먹기 위해 아픈 것을 참고 자지를 까 보였다. 감 한 개를 얻어먹으려고 말 타기 놀이의 말 노릇을 한나절 했다. 끝없는 배고픔 속에서 배를 채울 수 있다면 무슨 일이든 하려 들었다. 그러나 그것도 열서너 살까지였다. 열다섯이 넘으면서부터는 이뿌리가 아플 지경으로 이빨을 앙다물기 시작한 것이다.

"만석이, 만석이, 나 잠 살려 주소. 내 논밭 다 줄 팅께 나 잠 살려 주소."

누군가는 손바닥이 불이 나도록 비벼대며 숨이 넘어갔다.

"만석이, 아녀, 아녀, 부위원장님, 나허고 춘부장 어르신네허고는 삼십 년 친구였지라우. 나 잠 살려 주씨요, 나 잠……."

누군가는 펑펑 눈물을 쏟으며 마룻바닥을 뺑뺑이를 돌았다.

"부위원장 동무, 부위원장 동무, 부위원장 동무……."

revolutionary cause.

As he fled, Man-sŏk kept to the remote and sparsely populated villages where the People's Army seldom appeared, lest he be forcibly conscripted along with all the other able-bodied men. Every night as he slept he was plagued by nightmares, visions of two naked bodies moving as one, and then the same bodies slithering in a sea of blood and intestines. The image wouldn't stop popping into his head; it appeared, even when he was eating, sickening him.

Man-sŏk had been laying low for a month when the news came that the North Korean People's Army had been defeated on the battlefield and were retreating into the mountains. He pondered what might have happened to him, if not for the incident in his hometown. The world had turned completely upside down yet again. Without a doubt, the Chŏng men who'd been able to escape would be back with revenge on their minds. He would've had no choice but to run away with the People's Army.

The war had drawn to a close, but its aftermath was still unfolding. Clean-up operations began, just as they did at harvest time when the threshing was over. The starving communists who'd holed up in

누군가는 입술을 푸들푸들 떨며 더는 말을 못했다.

누군가는 생똥을 쌌고, 누군가는 질퍽하게 오줌을 쌌고, 누군가는 팔다리가 떨리다 못해 뻣뻣이 굳어져 버렸다.

그 누구 하나 며칠 전까지 가졌던 그 당당함, 그 거만함, 그 거드름, 그 위세를 그대로 지니고 있는 사람이 없었다. "요 개만도 못헌 쌍놈아, 니놈이 감히 누구헌테 요런 못된 짓을 혀!" 이렇게 호령을 하는 사람이 하나라도 있었더라면, 그 사람은 차라리 살려 줬을지도 모른다.

그들의 망령이 막아서라도 다시는 올 수 없는 땅이 된 것이라고 생각하며 만석은 강을 등지고 어둠 속을 빨리 걷기 시작했다.

만석 영감은 연상 눈물을 훔치며 변두리 고아원에서부터 번화가까지 걸어 나오느라고 서너 시간이 걸렸다. 수중에 동전 한 닢 남아 있지 않아 걸을 수밖에 없었다.

눈여겨보아 두었던 육교를 찾아냈다. 난간을 붙들고 힘겹게 육교를 오른 영감은 검정 고무신 한 짝을 벗었다. 그리고 양쪽 계단이 갈라지는 육교 바닥에 쪼그리고 앉았다. 검정 고무신 한 짝은 그 앞에 놓여졌다.

당장 하루 한 끼는 입에 풀칠을 해야 했고, 고향으로 갈

the mountains showed their faces in the villages once in a while, but only at night. During the days, the restored masters were busy rooting out Red collaborators.

"I don't need to tell you how it was. Some never came down from the mountains, and others who loitered behind were seized. They suffered the same fates they'd doled out to their enemies."

As if not wishing to talk any further, Hwang just shook his head over and over.

Man-sŏk drew a sigh as long as a river and set off walking slowly through the darkness. As Hwang had said, he had no choice but to go to some far off place and stay there. Nothing had been gained, and nothing remained, not for him. He felt empty and dazed.

He had always dreamed of going to the place called "school."

But they told him learning wasn't for just anybody. Certain things had been set aside for peasants to do, like cutting firewood, carrying loads on an A-frame, and tending the cows. While the Chŏng children giggled in the shade, eating melons until their bellies nearly burst, he had to run along the dikes of the rice paddies in the blazing sun, shouting to

차비는 마련해야 했다.

이제 노동은 할 수가 없었다. 어느 노동판에서고 일거리를 주지 않았다. 주름투성이가 된 파삭 쭈그러진 얼굴도 얼굴이었지만, 이미 어깨가 축 늘어져 한눈에 노동판꾼의 몸이 아닌 게 표가 났다. 혹시 인정이 많거나 아니면 풋내기 현장 감독이 일거리를 떼 준다 해도 감당할 능력이 없었다. 전신이 풀려 버린 데다가 억지로 힘을 쓰고 나면 으레 피가 넘어오는 것이었다.

영감은 고개를 푹 수그린 채 눈을 감고 있었다. 그런 영감의 몰골은 영락없이 거지였다.

고무신에 동전이 얼마나 모아지는가에 대해서는 영감은 아예 관심이 없었다. 영감의 마음은 어느덧 고향으로 가 있었다. 영감은, 죽을 날이 가까워져서 그러는 것이려니 했다. 언제부턴가 부쩍 그곳으로 마음이 쏠리는 것이었다.

아무것도 남은 것이 없는 땅이었다. 반겨 줄 얼굴 하나 없는 땅이었다. 있다면 험악한 과거만이 있을 뿐이었다. 그런데도 한사코 마음이 쏠리는 것은 무슨 까닭일까. 아무리 생각해도 그런 자기의 속을 알 수가 없는 일이었다.

공사판을 따라 이 년인가 떠돌았다. 새로 벌어진 간척

scare away the birds feeding in the fields. In winter-time, he always had the job of carrying the Chŏng children's bookbags when they went to school. They had clothes several layers thicker than his and wore warm gloves, but they complained that their hands got too cold to carry the books themselves.

The Chŏng children offered him two rice cakes if he would peel back the foreskin on his penis and let them watch it snap. It was painful, but he did it. For a single persimmon, he was a horse, letting them ride on his back all day long. He was willing to do anything if it meant appeasing his relentless hunger. But that was only until he was thirteen or fourteen; after that, he would simply grind his teeth until they ached.

"Man-sŏk, Man-sŏk, please don't kill me! My land is yours! Just let me live!"

Some kept on praying to their last breath, rubbing their palms together so hard and so long that it seemed they would surely burst into flame.

"Man-sŏk, I mean, Deputy Chairman of the People's Committee, sir, your father and I have been friends for thirty years! Please don't kill me! I'm begging..."

Some burst into tears and writhed about on the

지 공사장을 찾아가다 보니 고향 땅이 백 리 조금 넘는 거리에 있었다. 처음엔 혹시 아는 얼굴이라도 만나게 될까 봐 다른 일터를 찾아 나설까도 했다. 그러나 공사장 여건이 선뜻 딴 데로 발길을 돌리지 못하게 했다. 간척지 공사는 우선 그 기간이 길어서 좋고, 대개 관에서 하는 일이라 일당이 제때제때 나오는 이점이 있었다. 몇 번을 망설이다가 될 대로 되라는 심정으로 주저앉고 말았다.

이 개월이 지나고 삼 개월이 지나도 아는 얼굴은 하나도 만나지지 않았다. 그렇게 되니 마음이 슬그머니 동하는 것이었다. 황 서방이라도 한번 만나 보고 싶은 생각이 일어난 것이다. 그 생각이 한번 머리를 들게 되자 마음은 자꾸만 설레발을 치기 시작했다.

노동판에도 사람은 얼마든지 있었다. 몸뚱이를 부려 하루 세 끼 목구멍을 채우는 같은 처지의 사람들이 많았다. 그러나 그들에겐 잘 구워진 고구마 맛 같거나, 눈 오는 날 구들장의 온기 같은 정이 없었다. 한 노동판, 같은 조(組)로 일을 할 동안은 그런대로 허물이 없는 듯하다가도 공사가 끝나고 뿔뿔이 흩어지게 되면 그 길로 까맣게 잊어버리게 되는 타인들일 뿐이었다. 떠돌이 인생들이란 으레 그런 모양이었다.

floor.

"Comrade Deputy Chairman, Comrade Deputy Chairman, Comrade Deputy Chairman..."

Some couldn't even speak a full sentence, their lips shook with such violence.

Some would shit, and some would piss a big puddle. Some trembled violently and then just froze solid.

Not a single one retained the power, arrogance or dignity they had exuded just a few days before. If anyone had dared to talk back with a "You worthless dog of a peasant, you can't do this to me!" Man-sŏk might even have spared his life.

Fear of those spirits alone was enough to banish Man-sŏk forever from that place. The river at his back, he hastened his pace through the night.

To get from the orphanage on the outskirts of the city to a main thoroughfare took the old man several hours. As he trudged along, Man-sŏk kept wiping the tears from his eyes. Penniless, he had no choice but to walk the whole way.

At last he found the overpass that earlier he'd thought promising. With difficulty he climbed the steps of the pedestrian bridge, hanging on to the

여자가 없는 것도 아니었다. 그러나 그 여자들은 오히려 남자들보다 더 허망한 그림자였다. 몇 푼의 돈으로 몸을 파는 그 여자들은 그 일이 끝나 버림과 동시에 아무 쓸모도 없는 살덩이로 변하고 말았다. 그 여자들과의 일은 아무리 되풀이해 보아도 발목밖에 안 차는 미지근한 목욕물에 들어선 기분이었다. 목까지 푹 잠기는 뜨끈뜨끈한 목욕물이 몹시 그리웠다. 언뜻 마누라의 몸이 생각났다. 전신이 흠빽 땀으로 젖으며 온몸의 진기가 다 빠져나간 것 같은 아련하고도 아슴하던 그 기분이 그리웠다. 그러나 그 그리움을 지체 없이 박살내고 달려드는 기억이 있었다. 벌건 대낮에 숙소에서 뒹굴던…….

황 서방을 만나 보고 싶은 것은 그런 마음의 정처 없음 때문인지도 몰랐다.

공사판은 일주일에 하루씩을 쉬었다. 그날은 너무 지루하고 답답했다. 술타령도, 투전판도 별로 마음이 끌리지 않았다. 정종이라도 한 병 사 들고 황 서방을 찾아가고 싶은 생각만이 마음에 가득했다.

만석은 꾹꾹 참다가 결국 점심때가 지나서 버스를 타고 말았다.

고향 마을을 삼십 리 앞둔 ㅂ읍에서 버스를 내렸다. 해

railing, and removed one of his black rubber shoes. He squatted down where the steps merged onto the bridge from both sides, the shoe set down before him. He needed money not just to eat, but for the fare to his hometown.

He wasn't fit to work anymore. No contractor would hire him. Apart from his weather-wrinkled face, his stooped shoulders made it evident that he lacked the strength for real labor. Even if a naive or compassionate foreman were to take him on, it would soon become clear that he was no longer capable of heavy work. Not only was his body totally run down, but also he would almost immediately start spitting blood, if he exerted himself at all.

His head bent down, the old man's eyelids were falling closed. He looked like nothing so much as a simple beggar.

He was utterly oblivious to the number of coins that had been dropped into his rubber shoe. In his mind, he had already returned to his hometown. To the old man, it seemed his last day on earth was at hand; he'd noticed his thoughts constantly gravitating to his birthplace.

Nothing was left for him there. Not a single face would greet him in that place. The only thing

가 지려면 얼마 남지 않은 시간이었다. 만석은 가게에서 정종 두 병을 샀다. 그리고 밥집을 찾아들었다. 국밥 곱빼기에다 소주를 시켰다. 밤길 삼십 리를 걷자면 든든하게 먹어둬야 했다.

"묘 쓰는 일이 안직도 안 끝났단 말이당가?"

"아, 그렇다니께."

"참말로 요상허네이. 난리 끝나 뿐 것이 원젠디, 이 년씩이나 묘를 쓴단 말인당가?"

"요 사람, 영 태평헌 소리만 혀쌓는구만이. 아, 죽은 사람 숫자가 을맨지 자네 몰라서 허는 소리여?"

"허긴 그때 인공 치하에서 반년만 더 끌었다면 정씨 문중 씨는 싹 말라 읎어질 뻔혔응께."

입으로 술잔을 가져가던 만석은 그대로 동작을 뚝 멈추었다. 몸이 뻣뻣이 굳어지는 것 같은 충격이 뒷머리를 때렸다. 만석은 눈만을 빠르게 굴려 두 남자의 얼굴을 살폈다. 전혀 안면이 없는 얼굴이었다. 만석은 자신도 모르게 파장이 심한 한숨을 내뿜었다.

"그러게 말이시. 국군이 그맘때만 혀서 싸움에 이긴 것은 정씨네헌테 큰 부조헌 거여."

"하먼, 하먼. 그란디 묘는 지대로 써지고 있는 것잉가?"

remaining there was his own terrible past. Why was his mind so irresistibly drawn to it time and again? It was a mystery to him.

For about two years he'd been drifting from worksite to worksite. One of the construction jobs he took happened to be less than a hundred *li* from his hometown. At first, fearing he might run into a familiar face, he considered leaving in search of work elsewhere. But because the job market was depressed, he found himself with no other options. The job was a land reclamation project and, as such, had several advantages. It would last quite a long time and wages would be paid promptly, since it was financed by the government. He had hesitated for a bit but finally decided to stay, telling himself the danger could be overcome.

Two months, then three months passed, and still nobody appeared who recognized him. He gradually found the form of his anxiety changing. Where he'd been afraid of discovery before, now he could only think about how much he'd like to see Hwang again, just once. The thought gave him not a moment of peace once it erupted in his head.

The worksite was full of people, of course. These

"워디가. 그 많은 사람덜이 굴비 엮듯 혀서 이 구뎅이 저 구뎅이 묻혀 뿐 것잉께 누구 뼈다구가 누구 뼈다군지 워찌 알 것잉가."

"참말로 환장헐 일이구만 그랴. 누구 뼈다군지도 모름시로 즈그덜 부모 것이라고 생각허고 이장을 허는 자손들 속이 워쩔 것잉가."

"금매 말이시. 그 효심들이 상 받을 만허다니께."

"근디, 정씨 문중은 그렇게라도 혼을 건진다 허고, 부역혔던 사람덜이나 그 일가 뿌시레기덜 망령은 워쩐디야?"

"아, 걱정도 팔짜여. 지금 정씨네 서슬이 시퍼런 이 마당에 부역허다 죽어 뿐 망령 걱정허게 되얐능가?"

연거푸 술잔을 비우고 있는 만석의 마음은 싸늘하게 긴장하고 있었다. 그만 자리를 뜨고 싶은 마음과는 달리 몸은 점점 더 무거운 무게로 아래로 내려앉고 있었다.

"내 말은 고런 말이 아니란 마시. 워쩌케 되얐거나 간에 한 품은 망령이 떠돌아댕겨서는 그 동네가 안 되야묵능다 그런 말이네."

"그렇다고 정씨 문중에서 그 웬수녀러 상것들의 묘를 써 줄 것잉가?"

"가당찮은 일이제. 무신 감투를 쓴 것도 아닌 그 멍청한

were men like himself, earning three meals a day with the sweat of their brow. But even with them, something was missing. In the company of real friends, one feels warm, as if sitting on a coal-heated floor on a snowy night. These fellow workers were chummy enough during the workday, but when the job ended they all scattered like leaves in the wind, not giving each other a second thought. Perhaps that was what it meant to be a drifter.

It wasn't that there were no women. But somehow the women were even hollower than the men. Those who sold their bodies for a paltry sum turned into nothing more than useless flesh as soon as their work was over. No matter how many times he lay coupled with such women, it was always like getting into a bathtub with lukewarm water that only covered his ankles. He longed to be immersed up to his neck in a steaming hot bath. Suddenly, he would remember his wife. He missed that sensation of being drenched in sweat, all strength drained from his body... but there was always a memory lying in ambush to do away with his longing. Those tangled bodies on the office floor in broad daylight...

This restless state of mind, perhaps, was what

점바구를 생매장헌 걸 보면 정씨네도 보통은 넘는 사람들이여."

"하먼, 말허먼 멀혀. 내놓고 말은 못 혀도, 워디 부역헌 사람들만 다 나쁘간디. 인자 정씨네도 맘덜 고쳐묵어야 헐 것이여."

"암만, 북은 쳐야 소리가 나고, 바람이 불어야 나무가 흔들리는 것 아니드라고."

……점바구, 왼쪽 이마에 동전만 한 점이 박혀 있던, 약간쯤 모자라는 것 같은 사내. 그는 제 세상이 왔다고 덩실거리며 대창을 꼬나 잡고는 시키는 일이면 무엇이나 해치웠다. 대창으로 가슴팍을 푹 찔러 놓고는 누런 이빨을 드러내고 헤벌쭉 웃는 것이었는데, 그런 그의 얼굴은 웃는 것이 아니라 성난 개가 으르렁 거리는 모습과 너무나 흡사했다. 그 섬뜩한 느낌의 표정을 사람들은 '개웃음'이라고 불렀다. 그 점바구가 생매장을 당했다는 것이다. 약간쯤 모자라는 탓으로 사태가 불리해진 낌새를 눈치채지 못했을 게 뻔했다. 점바구는 생매장을 당하면서도 개웃음을 웃었을까……. 술잔을 들어 올리고 있는 만석의 팔이 부들부들 떨렸다.

"워쨌거나 인자 공비가 안 내려옹께 살겄구만. 작년꺼

made him want to see Hwang once more.

On the construction job they got one day off a week. Those days were unbearably suffocating. Neither the bouts of drinking nor the gambling held any attraction for him. All he wanted to do was to sit down with Hwang over a couple of glasses of rice wine.

Man-sŏk suppressed his desire until after lunchtime, but in the end he found himself boarding the bus. He got off at the hamlet of B, some thirty *li* from his hometown. Dusk was approaching. He bought two bottles of rice wine at a shop and ducked into a small tavern. He ordered a large bowl of rice in broth and *soju.* The long night walk he faced called for a substantial meal.

"You mean they aren't done with the graves yet?"

"Yeah, that's what I said."

"That's bizarre, eh? How long's it been since the war? You telling me they're still working on the graves two years later?"

"Look, man, you talk like you don't know anything about it. You know how many of them were killed, don't you?"

"Yeah, true enough. If the Northerners had held power another six months, there wouldn't be a sin-

정만 혀도 어디 발 뻗고 편헌 잠 잘 수 있었더라고.”

“인자 에지간히 잽힌 모냥이여. 위원장 지냈던 수길이가 죽어 뿐 작년 시월 후로는 그 동네에도 이적지 한 번도 안 내려왔드랑만.”

“그라먼 그때 수길이허고 함께 죽은 그 얼굴이 몰라보게 잉끄레져 뿐 것이 소문대로 부위원장 지낸 만석이가 영락없는 것 아니었쓰까?”

“모르먼 몰라도 그럴껴. 그때 싹 죽어 뿌러서 발이 끊긴 것 아니겄어. 그때 수길이만 죽고 만석이가 살아 달아났드라먼 정씨 문중이 무신 험헌 꼴 또 당혔을지 아능가? 고 만석이란 물건이 예사 물건은 아니였등갑는디. 독허기가 독사 대가리 열 합친 것만 허다드만 그랴.”

“글씨 말이시, 열 살 안짝에 비얌을 꾸어 묵은 징헌 자석이람시로?”

“그러타느만.”

“근디 마시, 만석이 그 사람이 분주소장허고 즈그 마누래 줘여 뿔고 내빼 뿐 것허고 인민군이 봇짐을 싼 것허곤 보름이나 더 차이가 지는디…… 그라고 인민군헌티는 만석이가 총살감 죄인이 아니겄드라고? 그란디 워쩌케 또 한패가 되얐으까?”

gle Chŏng left above ground."

Man-sŏk froze, his *soju* glass halfway to his lips. It was as though he'd been hammered on the head. Swiftly, he rolled his eyes over to the faces of the men he'd overheard talking. They were total strangers to him. In spite of himself, he breathed a deep sigh of relief.

"That's the truth. The victory of the ROK Army came along at just the right time for the Chŏng clan."

"Indeed, indeed. So are things going okay with the grave moving?"

"No way. How in the world can they tell which bones are which, when so many bodies were packed like sardines in this hole and that hole!"

"Really, that'd drive anybody crazy. Think how they must feel! Trying to build tombs for their parents but never being sure whose bones they're burying."

"I'll say. Their filial piety is worthy of praise."

"Well, thanks to these efforts, at least the Chŏng dead may be able to rest in peace... but what about the souls of those on the Communist side? What of their families?"

"Don't you worry about it. With the Chŏngs back

"요 사람 참말로 답답허네잉. 속사정이 워쨌든, 넘 마누라 붙어묵는 놈이 잘못인가. 그런 놈 쥑인 남편이 잘못인가. 즈그덜도 속이 있응께 옛일 덮어 뿔고 다시 합친 것 아니겄어? 그라고 심이 달려 쫓기는 판에 한 사람 더 보태는 것이 워딘디. 만석이 같은 독헌 인종 하나 보태는 것은 예사 사람 열 보태는 폭이었을 것 아니라고?"

"그러컸구만, 그러컸어."

만석은 창백한 얼굴로 식당을 다급하게 나왔다. 그리고 황 서방 집과는 반대쪽으로 걷기 시작했다. 공사판 쪽으로 가는 차가 있어야 할 텐데 생각하면서.

공사판으로 돌아온 만석은 황 서방에게 주려고 샀던 정종 두 병을 다 마셔 버렸다. 그리고 나흘 동안 꼼짝을 못하고 앓아누웠다.

열 살 안쪽 나이에 뱀을 잡아 구워 먹은 일은 없었다. 구워 먹으면 어떨까 하는 생각은 많이 했었다. 소·돼지·개·닭은 다 먹는다. 메뚜기나 개구리도 먹는다. 그러면 뱀이라고 못 먹을 게 뭐 있을까 싶었다. 여름이 되면 뱀은 강변 갈밭이고 논이고 야산 풀섶에 흔했다. 아이들은 뱀을 보면 질겁하고 뺑소니를 쳤다. 그러다가도 누군가가 한 마리 잡기만 하면 너도나도 돌멩이를 들고 대드는 것

on top, why bother yourself about those wandering ghosts?"

Man-sŏk felt cold and tense as he drained one glass after another. His mind told him to fly away from there at once, but he felt his body sinking like a stone, deeper and deeper into some abyss.

"That's not what I meant. What I'm saying is, regardless of the cause, the village will suffer if restless souls are about."

"Even so, the Chŏng clan is not about to allow decent tombs to be erected for the rebel peasants who were their mortal enemies."

"True enough. Remember that half-wit everybody called 'Blotch'? He was a nobody, but the Chŏngs went ahead and buried him alive."

Blotch... the guy with the huge mole on his left temple... he had always been a bit screwy in the head. He'd danced about, singing that his world had come and was ready to carry out any order with his bamboo spear. Stabbing somebody viciously in the chest with that spear, he would smile, his yellow teeth making him look more like a growling dog than a man. That frightful face led people to call him "dog-grin." That very same Blotch, Man-sŏk was now learning, had been buried alive. Being

이었다. 으레 뱀은 온몸에 상처투성이가 되어 죽어야 했다. 그러나 아이들은 물러나지 않았다. 뱀을 토막 쳐 죽이지 않으면 밤이슬을 먹고 되살아나 새벽에 꼭 복수를 하러 온다는 것이었다. 되살아난 뱀은 자기를 죽이려 했던 아이들 집을 하나하나 찾아다니며 꼭 자지를 물어 죽인다는 것이었다. 그래서 아이들은 사생결단 돌을 던져 다 죽어 버린 뱀을 토막토막 끊어야 직성이 풀려 했다. 어떤 아이는 한 손으로 사타구니를 거머잡고 기를 쓰며 돌을 던지기도 했다. 그러나 만석은 돌을 던지지 않았다. 배가 고파 기운이 없는데 뱀을 죽이는 일에 기운을 쓸 필요가 없었고, 저것을 어떻게 하면 구워 먹을 수 있을까를 열심히 궁리하고 있었던 것이다. 강에서 잡히는 뱀장어라는 것의 맛은 기막혔다. 기름이 지글지글 끓는 뱀장어 한 쪽을 입에 넣었을 때의 그 고소하고 달큼한 맛, 이름이 비슷하니까 하는 생각에 몰두해 있곤 했었다.

수길은 빨치산이 되어 동네를 습격했다가 죽은 모양이었다. 그놈도 억세게 불쌍한 놈이었다. 홀어머니 밑에서 어쩌면 만석이 자신보다 더 배를 곯으며 살았을지 모른다.

"니기미, 요런 팔짜로 한평생 살아 보먼 멀 헐꺼. 엄니 땀새 사는 것이지. 엄니만 죽어 뿔면 나도 요런 염병헐 시

almost an idiot, he wouldn't have understood that the tables had been turned yet again. Had he flashed that dog-grin even as they piled the dirt on him? Man-sŏk's arm trembled visibly as he lifted the glass.

"At any rate, now that the Red guerrillas aren't coming down from the hills any more, life seems to be back to normal. Up until the first of the year, you couldn't sleep a single night with your legs stretched out."

"Looks like all of them have been caught by now. Since last October, when Su-gil, the local Communist chairman, was killed, the Reds haven't shown their face once in that village."

"Do you believe what they say? That the man who died with Su-gil, the guy whose face was smashed beyond recognition, was the Deputy Chairman, Man-sŏk?"

"No way to know for sure, but it seems very likely it was him. He must have been killed then, and that's why he never showed up again. If only Su-gil and not Man-sŏk was killed, who knows what would have happened to the Chŏng. They say that this Man-sŏk was no ordinary character. I'm told he was deadlier than ten vipers rolled into one."

상 고만 살란다."

기운 쓰기에는 안 어울리는 뼈대를 갖춘 수길은 곧잘 이런 말을 하곤 했었다.

그는 인민위원장이 되면서 그래도 생기가 나는 것 같았다. 그러나 마구잡이로 사람을 죽이는 것을 꽤는 괴로워했었다. 그런 그가 결국 고향 땅에서 죽어 간 것이다.

고향 사람들, 특히 정씨 문중 사람들에게는 자신은 이미 죽은 것으로 되어 있는 모양이었다. 그러면 자신의 생존을 알고 있는 것은 황 서방 내외뿐이다. 입 무거운 황 서방이 자신의 생존을 입 밖에 낼 리가 없었다. 자신은 이미 죽은 목숨인 것이다. 이제 고향에 남은 자신의 흔적은 아무것도 없다.

만석은 나흘 동안 앓아누워서 자신의 신세를 골똘히 생각해 보았다. 참 허망하고 어처구니가 없었다. 달라진 것이라곤 소작 농사꾼에서 떠돌이 막노동꾼으로 바뀐 것이었다.

만석은 다시는 고향 땅 가까이 가지 않기로 마음먹었다. 그 결심은 삼십 년이 가깝도록 지켜져왔던 것이다. 아무리 좋은 일판이 벌어져도 고향 쪽이면 아예 외면을 해 버렸다.

"Yeah. I heard the first time he caught and ate a snake he wasn't yet ten years old."

"So they say."

"But you know, wasn't it only about two weeks after Man-sŏk murdered his wife and the North Korean commander that the Northern forces fled...? And, wasn't he a criminal to the Red Army, someone they'd shoot on sight? So how would he have joined up with them again?"

"You really are dense. Whatever the real story is, who do you think is really in the wrong? The guy who stole another man's wife, or the husband who killed that bastard? Even the Reds knew what had happened. They probably decided to take him back and leave the past buried. Besides, they were on the run and another man would've come in handy. A viper like Man-sŏk would've been worth six ordinary men to them."

"You're right. That makes sense."

Man-sŏk left the tavern, his face as white as a sheet. He took off, walking in the direction opposite to that of Hwang's place. He hoped he could find a bus headed back to the construction site.

When he got back to the work site, he drank both bottles of rice wine he'd bought to share with

강변에는 저녁 안개가 어떤 슬픔의 흔적처럼 자욱하게 번져 나가고 있었다. 무거운 듯 어깨를 늘어뜨리고 선 영감은 오래 전부터 갈대숲으로 번지는 안개의 꿈틀거림을 하염없이 바라보고 있었다.

지금도 저 갈숲에는 참게가 그리도 많을까. 어렸을 적에는 구워 먹었고 나이가 들어서는 술안주로 그만이었지. 소주 한잔을 꺾고 진간장에 담근 그 털북숭이 참게 다리를 씹는 맛이란…….

영감은 군침을 삼키며 손바닥으로 입을 훔쳤다. 손바닥의 꺼칠한 느낌만 입 언저리에 무슨 흉터처럼 선명하게 새겨지는 기분이었다. 영감은 허전한 기분으로 손바닥을 내려다보았다. 못이 박이다 못해 자디잔 금을 그으며 터진 손바닥. 굳어진 군살이라서 그런지 어지간한 것에 찔려서는 아픔을 느낄 수가 없었다.

영감은 가늘고 길게 한숨을 쉬었다. 손바닥을 내려다보고 있는 눈에 안개빛을 닮은 우수가 서렸다.

긴 세월이야. 빠르게 달아난 세월이야. 허망한 세월이고…….

영감은 입꼬리가 처지도록 입을 꾹 다물며 눈길을 다시 강변으로 옮겼다. 안개는 흡사 살아 있는 것처럼 질펀한

Hwang. For the next four days he was sick in bed.

He had never once caught a snake to roast and eat when he was a kid. The thought had entered his mind often enough. People eat cows, pigs, dogs and chickens. They even eat grasshoppers and frogs, so why not snakes, he used to tell himself. In the summertime, the snakes had been everywhere along the riverbank: in the bamboo groves, in the rice paddies, and hiding in the grass on the hillsides. The children had been terror-stricken, running away at the mere sight of a serpent. Whenever anybody had trapped one, they'd all wanted to be the first to throw rocks at it. The snake had always ended up dead, crushed by the stones. The kids, however, hadn't been happy with leaving it at that. They'd believed that unless you cut a dead snake into pieces, the night dew would bring it back to life so that by dawn it'd be seeking revenge. It was said that the revived snake would appear at the house of each boy who'd stoned it and kill him by biting him on the cock. And so naturally, the kids always cut the snake into pieces after the stoning. Some boys guarded their crotches with their hands while they threw rocks, but Man-sŏk had never once killed a snake. Always hungry, he had seen no

갈대밭과 넓은 강폭을 먹어 가고 있었다.

저 갈대밭이 없었더라면…….

영감은 몸을 으스스 떨었다. 막상 강을 앞에 하고 서니 그 일은 꼭 어제 일어난 것처럼 그동안의 세월의 간격을 허물어뜨리고 다가섰다.

안개는 그냥 퍼지고 있는 게 아니었다. 엷은 어둠을 한 자락 한 자락 깔아 나가고 있었다. 영감은 등줄기가 서늘한 한기를 느끼며 주위를 둘러보았다. 산등성이의 윤곽이 흐려 보일 만큼 어두워져 있었다. 영감은 눕고 싶은 무거운 피곤과 함께 시장기를 느꼈다. 이제 그만 주막으로 들어가고 싶었다.

옛 자리에 그대로 있는, 지붕만 슬레이트로 변한 왼편의 주막을 향해 영감은 더디게 걸음을 옮겼다. 이 꼴이 되어 버렸는데 어쩌랴 싶으면서도 어느 만큼 어두워지기를 기다렸다. 어찌할 수 없이 뼛속 깊이까지 스며 있는 죄의식이었다.

황 서방은 살아 있을까. 살아 있다면 칠십이 넘었을 것이다. 마누라한테 주막 일을 맡기고 자기는 나룻배를 저었었다. 추우나 더우나, 한밤이나 새벽이나를 가리지 않고 한 사람을 위해서도 나룻배를 띄우던 황 서방이었다.

point in using up his energy in that way. Instead, he was busy planning ways to cook and eat it when the others were through with it.

The river eels had an indescribably good taste, sweet and rich. Snakes and eels looked almost the same to him, so he imagined... It seemed that Su-gil had become a guerrilla only to be killed during a raid on the village. His fate, too, had been unhappy. Living alone with his mother, he might have grown up even hungrier than Man-sŏk.

"Screw it, what do I have to look forward to in this life? I live only for the sake of my mother. When she dies, I'm gonna put an end to this damn life myself."

Such things had often been heard from Su-gil, whose physique wasn't built for hard work. When he became Chairman of the People's Committee, it had been as if he was born anew. All the same, the reckless butchering of so many troubled him. In the end, he too met his death there in his hometown.

The Chŏng family apparently believed that Man-sŏk was dead. If so, the only ones who knew he was still alive were Hwang and his wife. Hwang could be counted on to keep his lips buttoned—he'd never whisper a word about Man-sŏk's being

항시 웃는 얼굴인 그는 이 세상에 싫은 사람도, 미운 사람도 없는 것 같았고, 그래서 감골·학내·죽촌 마을의 그 어떤 사람이든 황 서방 내외를 아끼고 감쌌다. 그런 황 서방이 처음으로 자신에게 눈을 치뜨며 소리를 높였었다.

"자네 워째 이러능가. 자네 미쳤능가? 시상이 워찌 변혔거나, 시국이 워찌케 달라졌거나 간에 사람이 변허먼 못쓰는 법이여!"

"황샌, 말조심허씨요! 황샌도 앞장서야 할 사람임스롱 무신 말을 고렇게 허씨요!"

"어이, 내 말 잠 들어보소. 일정(日政) 때 앞잽이 놀이허던 사람덜 꼭 못 봐서 그러능가?"

"멋이 워쩌고 워째라? 아, 지끔이 일정 때허고 똑같은 줄 아씨요? 나 마지막으로 한마디만 허니께 귀때기 활짝 열고 똑똑허게 들어 두씨요잉. 지끔 헌 말 황샌이니께 안 들은 것으로 허겄소. 한 번만 더 고런 소리 허먼 싹 보고허고 말 팅께 그리 아씨요."

황 서방은 입을 헤 벌린 채 아무 대꾸도 하지 못했었다.

황 서방이나 아버지는 그때 이미 세상살이가 어떤 것인지를, 한목숨 살아가는 뜻이 어디 있는지를 환히 알고 있었는지도 몰랐다. 둘이 다 순리로 살아야 한다고 했다. 그

alive. For all practical purposes, he was a dead man. Not a trace of him remained in his hometown.

In bed for four days, Man-sŏk reflected back on his life. It had all been absurd, all utterly senseless. He had merely changed from a tenant farmer into a drifting manual laborer.

Man-sŏk made up his mind never again to go anywhere near his birthplace. It was a vow he would keep for over thirty years. No matter how lucrative a job opportunity might be, if it was too close to that place, he would steer himself clear of it.

Evening mist was wafting along the riverside like the shadow of a certain sorrow. The old man stood with his shoulders drooping heavily, peering for a long while through the mist into the bamboo groves.

Will that grove still be full of crabs? As a boy he had roasted them, and as he had grown older, he came to love eating them when drinking liquor. There was nothing like biting into a crab-leg soaked in soy sauce after a gulp of *soju.* The old man swallowed hard, his mouth watering, and wiped his mouth with his palm. The rough feeling of his hand lingered on his mouth like some kind of scar. Feeling empty, he glanced down at his hand. The

순리라는 것이 무엇인지 알다가도 모를 일이었다.

이제는 황 서방도 어느 길목에서 마주친다 해도 서로 알아볼 수 없을 정도로 늙었을 것이다. 긴 물굽이를 이루며 흘러간 세월이었다.

영감은 징검다리라도 건너는 것처럼 약간 더듬거리는 듯한 걸음을 땅거미 속으로 내딛기 시작했다. 구부정한 어깨에 다 헐어빠진 가방이 매달려 있었다. 주막을 몇 발짝 남겨 놓고 영감은 걸음을 멈추었다. 그리고 기침을 하기 시작했다. 한 손은 입을 가렸고, 다른 한 손은 가슴께의 옷을 움켜잡고 있었다. 기침 소리는 전혀 생기가 없이 목구멍에서 맴도는 밭은 것이었다. 기침은 끊길 줄을 몰랐고, 영감의 몸은 점점 작게 오그라들고 있었다.

영감의 몸이 거의 주저앉다시피 하였을 때 기침이 멎었다. 영감은 숨을 헉헉대고 있었다. 이렇게 한바탕 기침이 휘몰아치고 지나가면 가슴은 다 찢어진 창호지 문처럼 너덜거리는 느낌으로 견디기 어려운 열에 들끓었다. 전신에 땀이 죽 흐르고, 오한이 일어나는 것은 그다음 증상이었다.

틀린 거야. 다 끝났어.

영감은 고개를 저으며 또 같은 생각을 했다. 기침이 한바탕 가슴을 들쑤시고 지나가면 영감은 또 한 걸음 다가

thick calluses were so parched that the skin was lined with countless cracks. His hands were so hard he seldom noticed any pain in them.

A long, thin sigh issued from the old man. As he stared down at the palm of his hand, there was a moist glint in his eyes that blended into the mist.

It's been a long time. The days have flown by swiftly... so little purpose, too...

The old man clenched his jaw tightly, the corners of his mouth jutting groundward, and his eyes drifted back toward the riverbank. The mist, like some predator, was devouring the bamboo and the water.

If only that bamboo grove had never been...

The old man shuddered. Now that he stood facing the river, the memory of the incident razed the wall of time and opened up before him as though it had occurred only yesterday.

The mist was not only spreading out, it was deepening the darkness layer by layer. A chill running up his spine, the old man gazed around him. It was getting dark enough to blur the silhouette of the mountains. He felt fatigued and hungry; he wanted to lie down. The time had arrived for him to go to the tavern.

The old man slowly walked along the path to his

선 죽음을 느끼는 것이다.

영감은 다리가 후들거려 무릎을 손바닥으로 짚고 더디게 일어섰다. 비릿한 냄새가 나는 것 같은 현기증이 강변에 퍼지는 안개처럼 아득하게 일어났다.

영감은 주막 문 앞에서 일단 멈춰 섰다. 뭐라고 인기척을 할까를 생각했다. 그러나 할 말은 떠오르지 않고, 젊은 황 서방의 순하디 순한 얼굴만 어른거렸다.

"기시요? 누구 없소?"

영감은 있는 힘껏 소리쳤다. 그러나 그 소리는 자신이 들어도 너무 힘이 없이 떨리고 있었다.

"누가 왔능가?"

한 남자가 헛간에서 나오며 두리번거렸다.

"……."

영감은 눈에 힘을 모았다. 저녁 어스름이 끼고 있긴 했지만 저쪽의 남자가 늙은이가 아니라는 건 직감할 수 있었다.

황 서방 아들일까?

영감은 불현듯 생각했다. 그 뚝심이 세던 녀석, 제 아비 대신해서 서툴게나마 노질을 하기도 했었다.

"큰 부조헌 기여. 저놈이 삼 년만 일찍 시상에 나왔어

left. The tavern still stood in the same place, and as he approached he noticed nothing different about it, except that the roof had been redone in slate. He wondered what they could possibly do to him when he was already in this condition, but he waited until it was dark to go in all the same. He couldn't help feeling a rekindling of the guilt that had seeped so deeply into the marrow of his bones.

Would Hwang still be alive? If he hadn't died, by now he'd be over seventy. He used to leave the tavern business to his wife and handle the ferry himself. In cold or heat, day or night, Hwang had never failed to ferry travelers across the river. A smile always on his face, he'd never even seemed to love or hate anyone in particular. Everybody in the hamlets of Kamgol, Hangnae, and Jukch'on had felt a warm affection for Hwang and his wife. Man-sŏk had been the first person to whom, with glaring eyes, he'd ever raised his voice.

"What's become of you? Have you gone mad? No matter how the world has changed, no matter how the times have changed, a man should not change!"

"Hwang, watch what you say! You yourself should have been one of the leaders. How can you possibly say such things?"

보드라고. 이쪽으로든 저쪽으로든 끌려가고 말았을 것잉께. 그랬으먼 내 애간장이 워찌 됐을 것잉가 말이시."

황 서방의 말이 생생하게 들리고 있었다.

"뉘시요?"

사십 대의 건장한 남자가 나직한 목소리로 묻고 있었다.

"저어…… 요새도 주막을 허능가요?"

영감은 뒤엉킨 여러 가지 물음을 밀쳐놓고 이 말부터 물었다.

"워디요. 다리가 생기고 나니께 나룻배가 소양없어지고 자연 주막도 시들해졌구만이라."

남자는 심드렁하게 대꾸하며 영감의 몰골을 달갑잖은 눈길로 훑어보았다.

"요 강 우로 다리가 놓였어라우?"

영감은 놀라움을 감추지 못하며 물었다.

"그것이 원제 일인디요. 이 고장을 떠난 지 영 오래되야 뿐 모양이지라우?"

남자는 새삼스러운 눈길로 영감을 찬찬히 훑어보았다. 영감은 반사적으로 방어 태세가 되었다. 그날 이후 삼십여 년 동안 겪어 온 감정의 어두운 굴절이었다. 그러나 영감은 그런 감정의 응고를 습관대로 겉으로는 전혀 드러내

"Look here! Don't you know how the collaborators ended up after liberation from the Japanese imperialists?"

"What's this nonsense you're spouting? How are these days anything like the Japanese occupation'? I'm going to tell you once more, for the last lime, so heed my words. I'll forget what you just said because it was you who said it. But remember, if there's a next time, I'll be the first to report you."

Hwang's mouth had hung wide open: speechless he'd been unable to reply.

Perhaps his own father and Hwang had each already known by that time what life was all about. Both of them had advised Man-sŏk that a man must live in accordance with the predestined order. The reason for that destiny had simply been something Man-sŏk was never been able to fathom.

Hwang must be so aged by now that he might be unrecognizable even if they passed each other in a narrow alley. So much time had meandered by, cutting its long unpredictable course through life. The old man started off along the dusty path. staggering along as if he were walking on stepping-stones, a worn bag hung over one of his stooped shoulders. A few steps before he reached the tavern, he

지 않고 입을 열었다.

"농새일이 싫어 젊은 나이에 봇짐을 싸분 것이요."

"그려요? 헌디, 돈은 잠 벌었능가요?"

남자는 비웃는 투로 물었다. 영감의 몰골은 돈과는 너무나 거리가 멀었던 것이다.

"혹시 지끔도 황 서방이 이 집에 사십디여?"

영감은 마음의 동요를 누르며 넌지시 물었다.

"황 서방이 누군디라?"

남자는 고개까지 흔들며 전혀 모르는 표정을 지었다. 순간 영감은 암담한 기분이 되었다. 이 남자는 집주인이 분명한데 황 서방을 모른다. 황 서방은 세상을 떠난 것일까, 아니면 어디로 이사를 간 것일까.

"멋이냐, 황순돌이라고…… 나룻배를 젓던……."

"아아, 전 주인 말이구만이라. 십 년도 전에 시상을 버렸구만요. 아들은 이 집을 우리헌테 넹기고 도회지로 떠나가 뿔고요."

영감의 귀에는 아무 소리도 들리지 않았다. 고향 땅을 찾아온 것이 아니었다. 황 서방을 만나러 온 것이었다. 정처 없이 떠돌면서도 마음이 고향 땅으로 쏠렸던 것은, 부모님 원혼이 떠돌고 있다는 가슴 아픔 말고도 황 서방이

stopped abruptly and began coughing. With one hand he covered his mouth, with the other he tugged at the neck hole of his shirt. The rasp of his cough was very weak, hanging in his throat. The old man couldn't stop coughing, and his frame seemed to shrink more and more.

By the time he managed to quit coughing, Mansŏk was almost on his knees, breathless. Such storms of coughing always made him feel like his chest was being ripped apart. An intolerable fever immediately followed, as usual. Soon his whole body was drenched as he broke out into a cold sweat; chills were always a part of it.

It's no use. It's all over.

The old man shook his head as the same old thoughts returned. Whenever he endured an onslaught of coughing, he could feel death coming one step closer.

His legs shook so badly that he had to brace himself with his hands, as he slowly got up from the ground. He felt a strange dizziness come over him, like the river mist, and a fishy smell descended upon him.

Once more the old man halted in front of the tavern. He searched for a way in which to announce

있었기 때문이다. 그런데 황 서방은 이미 십 년도 전에 세상을 떠났다는 것이다. 거렁뱅이짓을 해서 근근이 모은 돈이긴 했지만, 정종 한 병을 가방 속에 사 넣었던 것도 황 서방을 위해서였다.

"영감님은 워디로 가시는디요?"

집주인의 말에 영감은 정신을 차렸다.

"행여, 죽어 뿐 황샌 묏등이 워딘지 모르시겄소?"

영감은 물기가 번진 눈을 아슴하게 뜨며 물었다.

"글씨요, 잘 모르겄는디요."

남자는 무뚝뚝하게 대답했고, 영감은 연상 고개만 잘게 끄덕이고 있었다.

"그라먼 살펴 가시씨요."

집주인이 돌아섰다.

"나 시장혀서 그란디, 밥 잠 묵을 수 있겄소?"

영감은 집주인의 등 뒤에다 대고 힘없이 물었다.

"글씨요……."

"공짜 밥 묵자는 건 아니니께 염려는 놓으씨요."

"머 그것이 아니라, 찬이 벨로 읎어서…… 우선 듭시다."

집주인이 되돌아섰다.

himself, but he was at a loss for words. All he could think of was how kind Hwang had been in the old days.

"Hello! Anybody here?" cried the old man at the top of his voice.

But the sound was feeble, and he himself noticed how his voice trembled.

"Somebody out there?"

A man came out of a nearby barn, looking all about.

"..."

The old man gathered his strength to focus his eyes. Although the light was failing, he could make out that the other man was by no means old.

Could it be the son of Hwang?

Out of the blue, the thought popped into his head. He pictured the little boy who had stubbornly insisted on helping his father even though he had been unable to row the ferry very well at all.

"It was a blessing for us. Imagine what would've happened if the boy'd been born three years earlier. Then he would've been old enough to be drafted by one side or the other. If that'd happened I don't think I could have stood the worrying."

Hwang's words flashed through his memory.

사방은 어둠이 완연해져 있었다. 영감은 강변을 내려다보았다. 흡사 살아 있는 것처럼 뭉클뭉클 피던 안개의 자취는 암회색 어둠 속에서 찾을 수가 없었다. 황 서방만 있었더라면……. 영감의 가슴에는 허전한 슬픔이 강변을 덮던 안개처럼 퍼져 나가고 있었다.

"머 허씨요, 영감니임. 얼렁 들오씨요."

집주인이 불렀고,

"소피가 급혀서……."

영감은 얼버무리며 사립을 들어섰다.

마침 밥때여서 그런지 밥상은 금방 들어왔다.

"쇠주 한잔헐 수 있겄소?"

영감은 숟가락을 들 생각도 안 하고 술부터 찾았다. 그러면서 가방에 고이 간직해 온 정종을 생각했다. 황 서방과 마주앉아 마시려고 했었다. 지칠 만큼 지치고 시들 만큼 시들어 버린 감정과 육신을 달래며 한잔씩 하려고 산 술이었다. 자신의 평생을 통해서 정종이란 값비싼 술을 산 것은 이번으로 세 병째였다. 처음 두 병도 황 서방에게 권하지 못했고, 이번에도 마찬가지가 된 것이었다.

영감은 소주를 잔에 넘치도록 부어 단숨에 마셨다. 싸하고 짜릿한 소주 기운이 목줄기를 타고 내리는 느낌에

"Now, who might you be?" asked the man, sturdily built, apparently in his forties or so.

"Well... I was wondering if the tavern is still open here?"

Man-sŏk decided to begin with this simple question, clearing away the tangled thoughts that had been oppressing him.

"Why, no. When the new bridge came along, there was no need for a ferry and the tavern dropped by the wayside, too," replied the man casually, skeptically looking the old man over from head to toe.

"You mean they built a bridge over this river?" asked the old man, unable to conceal his astonishment.

"It's been there for ages. Must've been a long time, indeed, since you last visited this place."

He scrutinized Man-sŏk anew, instantly putting the old man on the defensive. It was a reflex, an expression of the sedimented emotions of the past thirty years. But the old man, as was his habit, hid his inner feelings, not even opening his mouth.

"I got sick and tired of farming and took off at an early age."

"Really? Were you able to earn a good living?" asked the man in a jeering tone. The remote look

영감은 눈을 지그시 감았다. 바람에 떠밀려 정처 없이 떠돌고, 구름을 이고 덧없이 보낸 세월 속에서 그래도 변함없이 곁을 지켜 준 건 이 소주 맛뿐이었다.

"자아, 한잔 받으씨요."

주인에게 잔을 내밀었다.

"워디요, 묵고 싶음사 내가 따로 묵제 워째 손님 술을 받아묵겄소."

주인은 팔을 내저으며 사양했다.

"보씨요, 술 한잔 주고받는 인정꺼정 고러크름 야박허게 토막치지 마씨요. 내 꼴 보면 다 알겄지만 술 두 잔 낼 돈도 읎는 신세요. 얼렁 받으씨요."

영감은 쓸쓸한 표정으로, 그러나 힘찬 어조로 말했다.

"그라먼……."

주인은 잔을 받았다.

술을 따르는 영감의 손이 잘게 떨렸다. 그러나 술이 잔에 다 찼을 때 손은 정확하게 술병을 거둬 올렸다.

"영감님, 나룻배럴 찾는 걸 보니께 죽골께로 가는 참이었능가요?"

주인이 잔을 내밀며 물었다.

"……."

on the old man's face seemed distant indeed from any question of money.

"Is Mr. Hwang by any chance still living in this house?" Man-sŏk inquired, suppressing his agitation.

The man shook his head, evidently unable to make heads or tails of the question. At this response, the old man felt utterly lost. The man was apparently living in this house, and he showed no sign of knowing who Hwang was. Had Hwang died? Had he moved away?

"Wait a second. His name is Hwang Sun-dol... He used to run the ferry..."

"Oh, yes. The former owner of this place, you mean. It's been more than ten years since he passed away. His son sold this place to us and left for the city."

The old man could no longer hear anything. He hadn't come back to see his birthplace. He'd come to speak with Hwang. The reason he'd been obsessed with visiting his home during his wanderings had not so much been unease about the restless souls of his parents, but the fact that Hwang was still there. And now, to hear that Hwang had been dead for more than a decade! The bottle he had in his bag, the bottle bought with money from

영감은 많은 생각을 모으는 듯 눈을 가늘게 뜨며 고개만 끄덕였다.

"여그 와 알았는디, 죽골서부텀은 왼통 정씨 문중 판입디다요."

"……."

영감은 여전히 고개만 끄덕였다.

"다리도 정씨 문중서 나서서 맨들었고, 얼매 안 있으면 중핵교 고등핵교도 맨든다고 허드만이라."

"……."

영감은 고개를 끄덕이며 담배를 빼들었다.

"허기사 국회의원이 나오는 판이니께 무신 일인덜 못 헐랍디요. 다른 성씨도 있긴 헌디 다 정씨네 그늘 덕에 사는 쪽박 신세들이지라우."

"헌디……."

영감은 무슨 말인가를 하려다 말고 술잔을 입에 털어 넣듯이 했다.

"무신 말씀인디요?"

주인이 영감을 물끄러미 바라보았다.

"헌디…… 정씨 문중 체(중심)를 잡아 가는 사람덜은 누굽디여?"

panhandling—that had been for Hwang.

"Where are you heading, old man?"

The old man returned to his senses.

"Do you by any chance know where Hwang was buried?" asked the old man, his eyes moist with tears.

"Don't really know" was the curt answer.

The old man nodded and kept nodding.

"Well, good-bye, then."

The man turned his back.

"I'm so hungry. Could I trouble you for a bite to eat?" the old man asked weakly.

"Well..."

"I'm not asking for a free meal, don't worry about that."

"It's not that. It's just that we haven't got much but rice. Let's go inside and see."

The man turned once more toward the house.

It was now completely dark. The old man gazed down the river. The lively envelope of mist had disappeared into the grayness of the night. If only Hwang were still around... A hollow sadness pervaded his heart like the river's mist.

"What are you waiting for, old man? Come on in," called the man.

"그야 배웠다는 내 나이 또래 사람덜이지라우. 노인네덜이 읎는 건 아니지만 다 뒷전에 나앉은 모양입디다. 그란디, 소문으로 들응께 그 노인네덜이 벨로 대접을 못 받는다는 말이 있드만이라."

"워째서?"

"덜 똑똑혀서 그런다는디, 진짜배기 똑똑헌 사람덜언 난리 통에 다 죽어 뿌렀답디다."

"……."

영감은 굳어진 표정으로 벽을 응시하고 있었다.

"정씨네가 난리 통에 죽긴 억수로 죽은 모양이드만요. 추석, 설 빼놓고 정씨 문중에서 젤 큰 행사가 칠월 하순에 드는 합동 제산디, 그 구경거리가 참말로 볼 만허드랑께요."

"……."

영감은 눈을 꼭 감은 채 담배만 깊이깊이 빨아들이고 있었다.

"세도깨나 부리던 정씨네가 난리가 나는 바람에 하루아침에 상것들 손에 잽혀 파리 목숨이 되얐으니, 그 한이 풀릴 리가 읎잖겄소? 그 난리 통에 상것들 안 날친 디가 읎었는 모양이제만, 여그 정씨 문중 동네서는 유별났드람서

"I need to take a piss..." mumbled the old man as he stepped through the gate.

The meal table was presently brought in; it was around suppertime and perhaps it'd been waiting.

"Could I have a glass of *soju*?"

Before even thinking of lifting a spoon, he first asked for a drink. Simultaneously, his mind fixed on the precious bottle concealed in his bag. It was the bottle he'd bought to share with Hwang, hoping to find some consolation for his exhausted body and mind. It was only the third time in his life that he'd bought the expensive rice wine called *Jeong-Jong*. He'd been unable to share the first two bottles with Hwang, and this time, too, things hadn't gone as planned.

The old man poured his glass full of *soju* and drained it in one gulp. At the piercing feeling of the liquor running down his throat, he shut his eyes. In all his years of aimless drifting, swept before the wind under cloudy skies, the only thing that had never changed was the taste of *soju*.

"Here, please accept one glass from me."

He offered his glass to the other man.

"Why, no. If I want a drink I'll get my own and not take one from what you paid for."

요? 영감님은 그때 그 징헌 굿을 보셨습디여?"

"아니, 아니여……."

영감은 담배를 비벼 끄며 고개를 세차게 내저었다.

"그때 워디서 살았습디여?"

주인이 영감의 얼굴을 지그시 들여다보듯 하며 물었다.

"난리 전에 일찌감치 여그럴 떠나 부렀소. 그렁께 난리통에 일어난 일은 암것도 모르겄소."

영감은 잘라 말했다.

"참 볼 만헌 굿이었능갑든디. 영감님은 존 귀경거리 놓쳤구만이라."

주인은 그때의 이야기를 듣게 될지도 모른다고 은근히 기대를 했던 모양이고, 그 기대가 깨져서 그러는지 실망하는 눈치였다.

"존 귀경거리는 무신 존 귀경거리였겄소. 사람 쥑이고 죽는 꼴 잘못 봤다 허면 평생 병 되는 법인디."

"그려도 그것이 워디 예사 귀경거리간디요? 상것덜 날치는 꼬라지가 을매나 가관이었겄소. 참 볼 만혔을 것이요."

영감은 더 이상 대꾸를 하고 싶지 않았다. 말끝마다 상것들, 상것들 하는 말이 몹시 비위에 거슬렸지만 탓하지

He waved his hands as he refused the offer.

"Come now. No need to be such a stickler when a fellow man just wants to share a glass. As you can see from the way I look, I can't afford to offer you a second drink. You needn't refuse the offer."

The old man, though he looked pathetic, spoke with firmness.

"If you insist..."

The man accepted the glass.

As the old man poured the *soju*, his hands began to shake. In spite of his shaking hands, the old man managed to fill the glass to its brim without spilling a single drop.

"Judging from your questions about the ferry, I gather you're on your way to Chuggol?" the man asked as he handed the glass back.

"..."

The old man just nodded, squinting as if in concentration.

"I didn't realize before I came here that the Chŏng clan owned so much land; starting in Chuggol it is all theirs."

"..."

Still, the old man only nodded.

"The bridge was the Chŏng family's idea. And I'm

말자고 했다. 이 사람이 무엇을 알랴 싶었던 것이다. 마흔으로 잡아도 열 살 적 일이고, 서른다섯으로 잡으면 다섯 살 적 일인 것이다. 이 사람은 그때의 죽이고 죽던 참혹한 일을 멀고 먼 옛날이야기로 재미있어 하고 있을 뿐이었다. 삼십 년의 세월은 그런 것이었다.

"잘 묵었소. 나 이만 가 봐야 쓰겄소."

영감은 힘겹게 일어섰다.

"날이 까빡 어두어져 뿌렀는디 괜찮을께라?"

"다 아는 길잉께로……."

영감은 술기운 탓인지, 기운이 없어서 그런지 휘청거리며 마당을 가로질러 갔다.

"어둔디 조심허씨요이."

다 헐어빠진 가방을 옆구리에 꼭 낀 채 휘청휘청 어둠 속으로 사라지고 있는 영감을 향해 주인은 소리쳤다.

영감의 시체가 다리 아래쯤에서 발견된 것은 다음 날 오전이었다. 다 헐어빠진 가방을 앞가슴에 꼭 껴안은 채로 굳어진 영감의 얼굴을 알아보는 사람은 아무도 없었다. 경찰이 신원을 파악하기 위해 소지품을 다 뒤졌다. 그러나 가방에서 나온 것은 몇 푼의 돈과 정종병 하나였다.

told they'll soon be building a high school, too."

Nodding still, the old man took out a cigarette.

"Now that a member of the Chŏng family is a legislator in the National Assembly, there's nothing they can't do. There are other family names as well, but they are all poor folk living in the shadow of the Chŏng."

"But..."

The old man had been about to say something, but he stopped himself and emptied the glass instead.

"What were you going to say?"

The man looked blankly at him.

"But... who are the leaders of the Chŏng clan these days?"

"Naturally, the men of my generation who have had an education. Not that there are no elders, but they seem content to take a back seat. Rumor has it that the older ones aren't much respected."

"Why so?"

"They say it's because they aren't too smart. The smartest supposedly died during the war."

"..."

The old man's expression was frozen; he just stared at the wall.

그 정종병에는 술이 반쯤 남아 있었다.

그대로 시체를 처리할 수 없게 된 경찰에서는 꼬박 하루 동안 시체를 길가에 놓아 두었다. 그리고 오가는 사람들에게 보게 했다. 그러나 영감을 아는 사람은 하나도 나타나지 않았다.

강에 사람이 빠져 죽었다는 소문을 듣고 많은 사람들이 모여들었다. 그 속에 주막집 주인도 끼어 있었다. 그는 소스라치게 놀랐지만, 다음 순간 침착해졌다. 괜히 아는 체했다가 경찰서로 불려 다니는 귀찮은 일 할 필요가 없다고 판단한 것이었다.

"어젯밤에 투신했다고 가정한다면 아마 저 위쪽의 옛날 나루터쯤이 투신 장소가 될 거야. 그래서 밤사이에 여기까지 떠내려온 거고. 그렇게 사건 조서를 꾸며서 처리하도록."

사복한 남자가 지시했고,

"알겠습니다, 반장님."

정복을 입은 경찰이 거수경례를 붙였다. 그리고 둘둘 말려 있던 거적을 쫙 펴더니 시체 머리에서부터 아래로 덮어 버렸다.

『유형의 땅』, 해냄, 1999(1981)

"Quite a number of the Chŏng perished in the war, it seems. Apart from New Year's and Chuseok, the biggest event of the year in these parts is the Chŏng family's memorial service for their ancestors. they do the rites on one day for all those who died in the war, and it's really a sight worth seeing."

"..."

The old man shut his eyes tightly and drew deeply on his cigarette.

"Just imagine. The Chŏng family, so used to their unlimited power, all of a sudden fell into the hands of the lowly peasants. Their lives became worth no more than the lives of flies. No wonder they're still full of bitter rancor. In wartime, there was no place in the country where the common folks didn't go on a rampage, but they say that here, the villagers' uprising against the Chŏng family went to extremes. Were you yourself around to witness those god-awful scenes?"

"No, no..."

The old man squashed out his cigarette and shook his head violently.

"Where were you living at the time?" the man asked, peering into the old man's face.

"I left here long before the war broke out. I can't

tell you anything about what went on then," the old man said bluntly.

"Must have been something worth seeing. You missed out on a real spectacle."

The man seemed to have been eager to hear the tales of those times and was disappointed to miss such an opportunity.

"How can you say it would have been a sight worth seeing? To have the bad fortune even once of witnessing people killing and being killed is more than anyone should have to bear in a lifetime."

"But still, it wasn't the kind of event that comes along every day. What a sight it must have been! The common folk rising in rebellion... I say, it must've been worth seeing."

The old man no longer felt like responding. The man's use of the words "common folk" irked him, but he decided not to make an issue of it. What could he know about it, anyway? He was too young. He couldn't be more than thirty-five or forty, so those events would have happened when he was five or ten. To him, the grisly scenes of murderous butchery were no more than an interesting story that had taken place once upon a time, long, long ago. That was the effect of thirty years.

"Thank you for the food. It's time for me to be on my way."

With difficulty, the old man lifted himself up.

"Will you be all right? It's pitch dark out there."

"I know the road well..."

Whether it was due to the drinking or just his weakness, the old man staggered as he crossed the yard.

"Take care in the dark!" the man shouted as Man-sŏk disappeared into the night, his worn bag hanging under his arm.

It was the next morning when the body of an old man was found in the shadow of the bridge. Nobody recognized his rigid face. A ragged bag was tightly clutched to his chest. The police searched through all his belongings in an effort to identify him, but all that was in the bag were a few coins and a bottle of *Jeong-Jong*. The bottle was half full.

Unable to simply dispose of an unidentified body, the police left it by the road for a full day, on the chance that passers-by might recognize the corpse. But nobody knew who he was. A rumor spread that a man had drowned himself and soon a crowd gathered. Among them was the man who lived in Hwang's old place. He was greatly startled at first, but regained his composure after a few moments. He reckoned there was no call to reveal his meeting with a nameless old man; it would only mean a bothersome visit to the police station.

"Supposing he jumped in the river last night, he probably hit the water somewhere around the old ferry crossing. He must have floated downstream during the night. Write up the report that way," ordered a man in civilian dress.

"Yes, sir," said a uniformed policeman, saluting.

They unrolled a straw mat and covered the body.

Translated by Chun Kyung-ja

해설

Afterword

한국전쟁과 분단, 저주받은 자들

고명철(문학평론가)

조정래의 소설을 읽는다는 것만으로도 소시민은 역사로부터 비껴나 있지 않고, 역사의 현장에서 고동치는, 소시민의 내면 한 켠에 자리하고 있는 시민적 양심과 만난다. 반공주의를 전가의 보도처럼 휘두른 국가권력의 전횡에도 불구하고 반공주의에 억압되지 않는 이념적 활달함으로써 역사와 삶의 진실을 추구하는 조정래의 소설은 불구화될 뻔했던 한국의 역사에 건강성을 회복시킨다.

조정래의 많은 작품들 중 「유형의 땅」(1981)은 정치적 이념의 대립으로 인해 한반도의 남과 북으로 나뉜 분단 시대의 역사적 상처에 주목하고 있다. 이 소설의 제목이 모든 것을 압축하여 보여 주듯, 작가에게 분단 시대를 살

The Korean War, the Division of the Country, and the Condemned

Ko Myeong-cheol (literary critic)

While reading Jo Jung-rae's novels, a petty bourgeois has to confront his own conscience as a citizen, a conscience that does not flinch from history but pulsates with it as history evolves. By openheartedly pursuing the truth of history and life, defying state tyranny that wielded anti-communism as if it was a trump card, Jo's novels have been restoring health to Korean history that could otherwise have been crippled. *The Land of the Banished* (1981) is one of many works by Jo that deal with the historical trauma of a country divided into two ideologically confrontational states. As the title of the story succinctly summarizes, Korea during this

고 있는 지금, 이곳은 바로 어떤 끔찍한 형벌을 받고 있는 저주받은 땅이다.

「유형의 땅」에서 주인공 만석은 고향을 떠나 타지에서 막노동꾼 삶을 살고 있다. 만석은 뿌리 뽑힌 존재로서 홀로 날품팔이를 하며 생계를 유지한다. 그러던 만석은 노동판에서 자신처럼 떠돌아다니는 삶을 살고 있는 순임이란 여성을 만나 살림을 차리고 쉰이 넘은 나이에 아들을 갖는다. 비록 늦은 나이지만 만석에게 행복이 찾아온 듯했다. 지난날 만석에게 행복은 꿈도 꿀 수 없는 것이었다. 그는 고향에서 가난과 계급적 차별의 삶을 살았다. 유년시절 그는 아이들과 참게 잡이를 하다가 사소한 싸움에 말려들면서 정참봉네 아이들을 흠씬 두들겨 패고 만다. 이 사건으로 만석의 아버지는 "정씨 문중에 끌려가 반죽음이 되도록 얻어맞고", "정씨 문중의 소작을 잃어버린 생활"의 고통을 겪는다. 이렇듯이 지주와 소작인 사이의 관계는 경제적 차별에 그치지 않고 소작인에 대한 지주의 반인간적 행태로 이어진다.

만석은 이러한 현실에 대한 증오의 감정을 품는다. 지주라는 이유로 소작인의 삶을 함부로 하는 것에 대해 만석은 극도의 반감을 품은 것이다. 만석의 이러한 반감은

age of division is a land condemned to horrific punishment.

In *The Land of the Banished*, Man-sŏk, the main character, lives as a manual laborer after leaving his home village. An uprooted day laborer, he barely makes ends meet. He meets Sun-im, a woman who leads a similar life, moves in with her, and has a son by her when he is past fifty. It seems that happiness has finally come to him in old age, a happiness he could not even dream of in the past. In his home village he led a life of poverty and endured discrimination. When he was a child, he was accidentally involved in a fight and ended up beating up the sons of Official Chŏng, a landlord, during a children's crab-gathering excursion. After this incident, Man-sŏk's father was "taken to the Chŏng household and beaten nearly to death." He also lost his livelihood because the Chŏng family took away his tenancy. Landlords wielded absolute power over their tenants financially and otherwise, treating them inhumanely.

Man-sŏk develops a hatred of this reality, harboring extreme enmity towards the tyranny of landlords over their tenants. During the Korean War, he becomes a vice-chairman of the regional people's

한국전쟁 동안 인민위원회 부위원장이 되면서 지주를 향한 보복의 행태로 드러난다. 이 보복은 이성적 판단에 근거한 것이라기보다 개인적 원한에 의한 것으로, 만석은 유년시절 정참봉네로부터 받은 온갖 반인간적 수모와 모멸을 되갚아 주려고 한 것이다.

여기서 작가는 독자에게 묻는다. 만석의 이러한 보복 행위를 어떻게 생각해야 할까. 만석이 아닌 그 누구라도 자연스레 취할 수밖에 없는 행위라고 보아야 할까. 과거 지주에게 당한 억울하게 맺힌 한을 풀어내는 것이라고 만석의 보복 행위를 정당한 것으로 간주해야 할까. 독자는 이 같은 물음에 대해 여러 측면을 생각해 보아야 할 것이다. 우선, 지주와 소작인 사이의 관계가 경제적 차별뿐만 아니라 인간적 차별을 낳는 이른바 계급적 불평등의 문제를 생각해 보아야 한다. 다음으로 이와 같은 불평등의 문제가 온전한 방법으로 해결되지 않고, 한국전쟁처럼 정치적 이념의 극단적 대립의 문제가 생길 경우 이 불평등의 문제를 해결하는 방법은 정치적 이념의 지배가 우세한 쪽에 의해 해결되는 과정에서 뜻하지 않은 또 다른 문제를 낳는다. 지주와 소작인 사이의 오랜 계급적 차별의 문제가 원한의 감정에 지배되면서, 결국 정치적 이념의 대립

committee, turning his hatred of landlords into a retaliation not based on rational thinking but on his personal feeling of resentment. His goal is to pay them back for all the inhumane and humiliating treatment he suffered from the family of Official Chŏng.

The author here asks his readers how we should perceive such an act of retaliation. Could we see it as an understandable response, natural to every human being, including Man-sŏk? Could we consider his retaliation justifiable, a resolution of his feelings of resentment to which he is compelled because of the brutal treatment he received from a landlord in the past? The reader is invited to think about various ways to answer this question. First of all, we need to consider the problem of class inequality between landlords and tenants that breeds not only economic inequality but also personal humiliation and discrimination. Also, when this problem of inequality is not solved by due process but by an extremely violent confrontation such as the Korean War, this violent solution generates even more problems. Because people are subject to intense personal feelings of resentment resulting from age-old discrimination, feelings that are in turn intertwined with

의 산물인 한국전쟁의 와중에 서로의 원한을 '죽음과 죽임'의 형태로 풀고자 하는 반인간적 행태가 널리 퍼지기 마련이다.

이 같은 비이성적 광기와 같은 반인간적 행태는 만석이 그의 처와 그의 상관인 분주소장이 정사를 하는 장면을 목도하고, 이들의 파렴치한 행위에 대한 분노로 이들을 모두 죽이는 것을 통해서도 여실히 드러난다. 백주대낮에 일어난 이들의 정사를 목격한 만석에게 이성적 판단이 들어설 자리는 없었다. 이 사건 이후 만석은 고향을 떠나 노동판을 전전하면서 삶을 연명해 나가며, 만석의 부모는 고향에서 총살을 당했다.

말 그대로 만석에게 고향은 행복과는 거리가 먼 불행으로 가득 찬 곳이며, 만석네 삶의 뿌리를 뽑아 버린 죽음의 기운으로 가득 찬 곳이고, 마을 사람들을 지배하고 있는 원한의 감정이 가득 찬 곳이다. 만석에게 그곳은 다시 기억하기 싫은, 영원히 망각하고 싶은, '유형의 땅'이다. 고향에서 만석의 흔적은 아무것도 없다. 고향 사람들에게 만석은 죽어 잊힌 존재일 따름이다.

작가는 만석의 이 같은 비참한 삶의 이력을 통해 독자에게 말한다. 특히 작가는 작품의 말미에서 만석으로 하

opposing ideologies, they are dragged into a cruel chain of "killing and being killed."

This kind of brutality unleashed by irrationality is well illustrated by the scene in which Man-sŏk witnesses his wife having sex with his superior and kills them both in a rage. There is no room for reason for Man-sŏk when he witnesses his wife's betrayal. Afterwards, Man-sŏk leaves his home village and again wanders around as a manual laborer; meanwhile, back in the village, his parents are shot to death.

To Man-sŏk, his home village is literally a place unrelated to happiness and in fact full of unhappiness, a place where his family lost their lives, a place filled with the stench of death, a place where villagers are dominated by feelings of resentment. It is a place that Man-sŏk does not want to remember, that he wants to forget forever, hence his wandering in a land of the banished. No trace of Man-sŏk remains in his home village. To his fellow villagers, Man-sŏk is dead and forgotten.

The author sends a message to his readers through this story of a miserable life, especially by returning Man-sŏk to his home village at the end of the story.

여금 고향을 찾게 하고, 그동안 고향에서 일어났던 비극적 사건들을 전해 듣고, 스스로 고향에서 목숨을 끊도록 한 것을 통해 만석은 한국전쟁의 참상을 결코 망각하지 않았으며, 자신과 연루된 역사의 상처들을 외면하지 않았고, 자신의 삶과 같은 역사의 상처에 대한 치유가 아직은 온전한 방식으로 치유되지 않는다는 것을 독자에게 들려준다. 비록 만석은 죽음을 통해 '유형의 땅'으로부터 멀어졌지만, 오히려 만석의 죽음과 관련한 삶의 내력을 알고 있는, 한반도의 주민들이야말로 '유형의 땅'을 더욱 실감하고 있다. 분단 시대를 살고 있는 한반도의 주민들은 '유형의 땅'으로부터 자유롭지 못하기 때문이다.

By having him hear about past tragedies, and ultimately commit suicide, the author tells us that Man-sŏk never forgot the horrors of the Korean War, that he never escaped the historical traumas that affected him, and that those traumas have not yet fully healed. Although Man-sŏk left 'the land of the banished' through death, we, the inhabitants of the Korean peninsula who know the story of Man-sŏk, are still living in 'the land of the banished.' Inhabitants of the Korean peninsula will not be free from this 'land of the banished' as long as they live in an age of division.

비평의 목소리

Critical Acclaim

조정래의 문학에서 6·25전쟁의 상처를 보다 내밀하게 구체화시킨 것이 소설 「유형의 땅」이다. 이 작품의 주인공은 전쟁을 거치면서 삶의 모든 것을 상실하고 있다. 하나는 자기 삶의 터전이 되는 고향의 상실이며, 다른 하나는 자기 존재의 뿌리가 되는 가족의 해체이다. 그리고 바로 그 비극의 한복판에 실체가 없이 자리하고 있는 완강한 이념적인 증오가 엿보인다. 소설의 주인공은 전쟁 당시 고향에서 인민부위원장이 되어 반동의 숙청에 앞장선다. 그러나 전쟁이 끝나자 고향을 빠져나와 신분을 숨기고 전전한다. 끊임없는 부랑으로 이어진 그 삶은 이른바 부역자의 비극적인 최후를 보여 주는 마지막 초라한 죽음

The Land of the Banished embodies the trauma of the Korean War in a more intimate language than Jo Jung-rae's other works. The main character loses everything during the war. First he loses his home village, the foundation of his life, and then he loses his family, the very root of his existence. In the midst of this tragedy lies stubborn ideological hatred, a non-physical entity. The main character in this story, a vice chairman of a regional people's committee, plays an active role in the cleansing of reactionaries during the war. After the war, he leaves his home village and wanders the country, concealing his identity. Horrible destruction charac-

에 이르기까지 모두 처절한 파괴로 점철되어 있다. 작가 조정래는 「유형의 땅」에서 바로 그 개인의 삶의 처절한 파괴가 무엇을 의미하고 있는가를 질문하고 있다.

권영민

작가 조정래의 문학이 갖는 힘 중의 가장 중요한 것이 바로 이 역사적 구체성이다. 역사와 현실을 다루고 있는 작가들이 정작 역사를 다루면서도 관념으로만 해석하고 역사적 구체성 속에서 묘파하지 못하기 때문에 허망하게 끝나는 것과는 달리 그의 문학은 항상 이것이 뒷받침되고 있기 때문에 사회과학적 해석을 넘어선다. 천민자본주의의 역사성을 천착하면서 근거 없는 졸부가 저지르는 폭력과 횡포를, 공적 영역이 결여된 산업화가 빚어내는 물신숭배의 부박함을 비판할 수 있었던 그가 결코 놓치지 않는 역사적 구체성이 바로 분단 현실이다.

김재용

『태백산맥』(1989) 이전과 이후에도 견지되는 작가의 사회관과 역사관은 부정적인 현실과 모순 구조에 대한 깊은 통찰과 비판으로 요약된다. 친일분자들의 잔혹하고 부도

terizes this life of endless wandering until the bitter end, i.e. his tragic death as a communist collaborator. Jo Jung-rae is asking all of us what meaning such a horrible destruction of an individual's life could have.

Kwon Young-min

One of the most powerful aspects of Jo Jung-rae's writing is its historical concreteness. Many authors who try to deal with history and reality fail in the end because their depiction remains abstract, failing to concretely embody historical reality. Jo supports his story with a concrete understanding of history, and goes beyond the abstract theorizing characteristic of the social sciences. He achieves historical concreteness by never losing touch with the reality of a divided country, while criticizing the upstarts of pariah capitalism for their violence and tyranny and the frivolity of commodity fetishism, a result of industrialization without corresponding development in other public arenas.

Kim Jae-yong

The author's viewpoint, consistent before and after *Taebaeksanmaek* (1989), can be summed up as his

덕한 형태와 맞물린 애국지사들의 저항과 민중들의 시련에 관한 이야기는 『아리랑』(1995)에서도 마찬가지로 비판적이고, 친일세력들의 발호와 압축 성장을 이룬 수많은 역사 주체들의 엇갈린 행로를 보여 준 『한강』(2007)에서도 그러하다. 거기에다, 동구 몰락과 소연방 해체 이후 무기징역수 박동건과 윤혁의 엇갈린 행로를 다룬 『인간연습』(2006)도 실패한 이념을 넘어 한 인간으로 재생하는 경로를 제시하고 있다. 이 작품은, 이념 우위의 현실에 대한 환멸 속에 신념을 지키며 죽어 가는 박동건과 인간애에 대해 고심하며 새로운 모색을 시도하는 윤혁을 대비해서 보여주고 있다. 연합군의 노르망디 작전에서 찍힌 조선인의 사진 한 장에 대한 의문에서 시작된, 제국의 틈바구니에서 살다간 존재의 망각을 고통스럽게 일깨우는 희생자의 이야기인 『오 하느님』(2007)도 마찬가지이다.

유임하

profound insight into, and criticism of, miserable reality and a contradictory social structure. This is true of both *Arirang* (1995), a novel about the cruel and immoral behavior of pro-Japanese elements, the resistance of patriotic independence fighters, and the suffering of ordinary people, and *The Han River* (2007), a novel about the crisscrossing paths of pro-Japanese elements and historical leaders of the country's accelerated economic growth. In addition, *Human Practice* (2006), a novel about two parallel paths chosen by Pak Dong-geon and Yun Hyeok, two prisoners serving life sentences for their communist beliefs, explores the ways in which they revive as human beings beyond their failed ideological beliefs. In *Human Practice*, the paths of Pak Dong-geon, who chooses to die with his beliefs even after being disillusioned about the ideological reality of the country, and Yun Hyeok, who explores a new way, based on his love of humanity, are compared and contrasted. A similar theme is explored in *Oh, God* (2007), the story of a victim who has been forgotten in the fight between superpowers, a story that begins with a photograph of a Korean taken during the Normandy Campaign.

Yu Im-ha

조정래

작가 조정래는 1943년 전남 승주군 선암사에서 출생했다. 그는 어렸을 때부터 강인한 성격을 가지고 있었다. 하루는 그의 머리에 난 땀띠가 곪아 혹이 되었다. 그래서 그의 부모님이 그를 데리고 동네 한의원으로 간 적이 있는데, 한의사가 고름이 가득 찬 혹에 침을 꽂는 순간 그가 발작적으로 울음을 터뜨리며 한의사를 향해 주먹을 휘둘렀다고 한다. 그의 세 살 때 일이다.

오 년 후 한국전쟁이 발발하며 그의 가족은 남쪽으로 피난을 가야 했다. 그는 새로운 동네에서 그곳의 토박이 아이들과 신경전을 벌여야 했다. 수적으로 보나 무엇으로 보나 열세에 있던 그는 하지만 정신력에 있어서만큼은 그들에게 결코 뒤지고 싶지 않았다. 그는 굴복하지 않고 싸워 이기는 길을 택했다. 그는 다음과 같이 고백한다.

"나는 그들에게 이길 수 없었다. 코피가 터지기도 했다. 하지만 울어서 진 적은 없다."

조정래는 국민학교를 다닐 때 이미 최초의 자작문집을

Jo Jung-rae

Born in Sonamsa Temple, Sungju-gun, Chŏllanam-do, in 1943, Jo Jung-rae was a child of strong character. Once when he was only two, he had a heat rash, which became a lump. His parents took him to a herbal doctor, who tried to treat him with acupuncture. As soon as the doctor stuck a needle into his lump, he was known to have burst out crying and tried to punch the doctor.

Five years later, when the Korean War broke out, his family evacuated to the south. In the village to which his family had moved, Jo had to engage in a war of nerves against the native children. Although he was inferior to them in number and physical strength, he never yielded without putting up a good fight. He confesses, "I couldn't beat them. I frequently had a nosebleed, but I never cried."

Jo was interested in creative writing from his childhood, making a collection of literary works in elementary school and winning the first prize in a writing competition within his school. After moving to

만들었으며 글짓기에서 전교 1등상을 타는 등 창작에 깊은 관심을 가지고 있었다. 이후 아버지를 따라서 서울로 입성한 그는 동국대학교 국어국문학과에 입학해 1970년에 문단에 데뷔한다.

1970년《현대문학》에 단편「누명」이 첫 회 추천되었으며, 같은 해 단편「선생님 기행」으로 추천이 완료되어 등단했다. 1980년 중편「유형의 땅」으로 현대문학상을 수상, 1982년 중편「인간의 문」으로 대한민국문학상을 수상하였으며 그 외에도 한국의 걸출한 문학상을 수상했다. 한국 사람들의 체험과 정서가 생생하게 살아있는 그의 작품은 한국문단사에 한 획을 그었다는 평가를 받고 있다.

조정래는 데뷔 이후 끊임없이 작품을 쓰면서 어떤 문제든 간에 역사적인 맥락과 삶의 구체성 속에서 진실과 거짓을 판단하려고 애썼다. 그의 치열함이 독자들에게 고스란히 전달되었기 때문일까, 그의 소설은 독자들을 대상으로 설문조사를 실시할 때마다 '가장 감명 깊게 읽은 소설', '후배들에게 권하고 싶은 소설', '지금까지 살아오면서 가장 기억에 남는 책' 1위로 꼽히곤 한다.

Seoul with his father, he studied Korean literature at Dongguk University.

He made his literary debut through publishing "False Charge" and "A Teacher's Travel" in the literary magazine *Hyondaemunhak* (Modern Literature) in 1970. He won numerous prestigious awards including the 1980 *Hyondaemunhak* Award for his novella *The Land of the Banished* and the 1982 Korean Literary Award for another novella of his, *Door to Humans.* Critics agree that he made an important contribution to the history of modern Korean literature through his works known for their vivid description of the experiences and emotions of ordinary Korean people.

Jo has been a consistently prolific writer since his debut. He has also been trying to tell truth from falsehood within every problem he has dealt with, and to look at it in historical perspective and in the context of our everyday lives. Perhaps it is because his readers could feel his passion in his words that they have often selected his work as "the most moving novel," "a book to recommend to others," and "the most memorable book."

번역 **전경자** Translated by Chun Kyung-ja

현재 가톨릭 대학교 명예교수이다.

Currently a professor of emeritus at The Catholic University of Korea.

감수 **마야 웨스트** Edited by Maya West

리드 대학교를 졸업했고 2003년 한국 문학 번역원 신인상을 탔다. 현재 서울에 거주하며 프리랜서 작가, 번역가로 활동하고 있다.

Maya West, graduate of Reed College and recipient of the 2003 Korean Literature Translation Institute's Grand Prize for New Translators, currently lives and works in Seoul as a freelance writer and translator.

바이링궐 에디션 한국 대표 소설 005
유형의 땅

2012년 7월 25일 초판 1쇄 발행
2017년 3월 27일 초판 3쇄 발행

지은이 조정래 | **옮긴이** 전경자 | **펴낸이** 김재범
감수 마야 웨스트 | **기획** 정은경, 전성태, 이경재 | **책임편집** 김형욱
편집 신아름 | **관리** 강초민, 홍희표 | **디자인** 나루기획 | **인쇄·제책** AP프린팅 | **종이** 한솔PNS
펴낸곳 (주)아시아 | **출판등록** 2006년 1월 27일 제406-2006-000004호
주소 경기도 파주시 회동길 445(서울 사무소: 서울특별시 동작구 서달로 161-1 3층)
전화 02.821.5055 | **팩스** 02.821.5057 | **홈페이지** www.bookasia.org
ISBN 978-89-94006-20-8 (set) | 978-89-94006-24-6 (04810)
값은 뒤표지에 있습니다.

Bi-lingual Edition Modern Korean Literature 005
The Land of the Banished

Written by Jo Jung-rae | **Translated by** Chun Kyung-ja
Published by ASIA Publishers | 445, Hoedong-gil, Paju-si, Gyeonggi-do, Korea
(Seoul Office: 161-1, Seodal-ro, Dongjak-gu, Seoul, Korea)
Homepage Address www.bookasia.org | **Tel**. (822).821.5055 | **Fax**. (822).821.5057
First published in Korea by Asia Publishers 2012
ISBN 978-89-94006-20-8 (set) | 978-89-94006-24-6 (04810)

〈바이링궐 에디션 한국 대표 소설〉 작품 목록(1~75)

아시아는 지난 반세기 동안 한국에서 나온 가장 중요하고 첨예한 문제의식을 가진 작가들의 작품들을 선별하여 총 105권의 시리즈를 기획하였다. 하버드 한국학 연구원 및 세계 각국의 우수한 번역진들이 참여하여 외국인들이 읽어도 어색함이 느껴지지 않는 손색없는 번역으로 인정받았다. 이 시리즈는 세계인들에게 문학 한류의 지속적인 힘과 가능성을 입증하는 전집이 될 것이다.

바이링궐 에디션 한국 대표 소설 set 1

분단 Division

01 병신과 머저리-**이청준** The Wounded-**Yi Cheong-jun**
02 어둠의 혼-**김원일** Soul of Darkness-**Kim Won-il**
03 순이삼촌-**현기영** Sun-i Samch'on-**Hyun Ki-young**
04 엄마의 말뚝 1-**박완서** Mother's Stake I-**Park Wan-suh**
05 유형의 땅-**조정래** The Land of the Banished-**Jo Jung-rae**

산업화 Industrialization

06 무진기행-**김승옥** Record of a Journey to Mujin-**Kim Seung-ok**
07 삼포 가는 길-**황석영** The Road to Sampo-**Hwang Sok-yong**
08 아홉 켤레의 구두로 남은 사내-**윤흥길** The Man Who Was Left as Nine Pairs of Shoes-**Yun Heung-gil**
09 돌아온 우리의 친구-**신상웅** Our Friend's Homecoming-**Shin Sang-ung**
10 원미동 시인-**양귀자** The Poet of Wŏnmi-dong-**Yang Kwi-ja**

여성 Women

11 중국인 거리-**오정희** Chinatown-**Oh Jung-hee**
12 풍금이 있던 자리-**신경숙** The Place Where the Harmonium Was-**Shin Kyung-sook**
13 하나코는 없다-**최윤** The Last of Hanak'o-**Ch'oe Yun**
14 인간에 대한 예의-**공지영** Human Decency-**Gong Ji-young**
15 빈처-**은희경** Poor Man's Wife-**Eun Hee-kyung**

바이링궐 에디션 한국 대표 소설 set 2

자유 Liberty

16 필론의 돼지-**이문열** Pilon's Pig-**Yi Mun-yol**
17 슬로우 불릿-**이대환** Slow Bullet-**Lee Dae-hwan**
18 직선과 독가스-**임철우** Straight Lines and Poison Gas-**Lim Chul-woo**
19 깃발-**홍희담** The Flag-**Hong Hee-dam**
20 새벽 출정-**방현석** Off to Battle at Dawn-**Bang Hyeon-seok**

사랑과 연애 Love and Love Affairs

21 별을 사랑하는 마음으로-**윤후명** With the Love for the Stars-**Yun Hu-myong**
22 목련공원-**이승우** Magnolia Park-**Lee Seung-u**
23 칼에 찔린 자국-**김인숙** Stab-**Kim In-suk**
24 회복하는 인간-**한강** Convalescence-**Han Kang**
25 트렁크-**정이현** In the Trunk-**Jeong Yi-hyun**

남과 북 South and North

26 판문점-**이호철** Panmunjom-**Yi Ho-chol**
27 수난 이대-**하근찬** The Suffering of Two Generations-**Ha Geun-chan**
28 분지-**남정현** Land of Excrement-**Nam Jung-hyun**
29 봄 실상사-**정도상** Spring at Silsangsa Temple-**Jeong Do-sang**
30 은행나무 사랑-**김하기** Gingko Love-**Kim Ha-kee**

바이링궐 에디션 한국 대표 소설 set 3

서울 Seoul

31 눈사람 속의 검은 항아리-**김소진** The Dark Jar within the Snowman-**Kim So-jin**
32 오후, 가로지르다-**하성란** Traversing Afternoon-**Ha Seong-nan**
33 나는 봉천동에 산다-**조경란** I Live in Bongcheon-dong-**Jo Kyung-ran**
34 그렇습니까? 기린입니다-**박민규** Is That So? I'm A Giraffe-**Park Min-gyu**
35 성탄특선-**김애란** Christmas Specials-**Kim Ae-ran**

전통 Tradition

36 무자년의 가을 사흘-**서정인** Three Days of Autumn, 1948-**Su Jung-in**
37 유자소전-**이문구** A Brief Biography of Yuja-**Yi Mun-gu**
38 향기로운 우물 이야기-**박범신** The Fragrant Well-**Park Bum-shin**
39 월행-**송기원** A Journey under the Moonlight-**Song Ki-won**
40 협죽도 그늘 아래-**성석제** In the Shade of the Oleander-**Song Sok-ze**

아방가르드 Avant-garde

41 아겔다마-**박상륭** Akeldama-**Park Sang-ryoong**
42 내 영혼의 우물-**최인석** A Well in My Soul-**Choi In-seok**
43 당신에 대해서-**이인성** On You-**Yi In-seong**
44 회색 時-**배수아** Time In Gray-**Bae Su-ah**
45 브라운 부인-**정영문** Mrs. Brown-**Jung Young-moon**